Mr. Meeks

His Life & Times
1812-1867

by
Damian Hopkins

(Reproduced by David S. Larson)

Mr. Meeks
His Life & Times 1812-1867

ISBN-13: 978-1512340686
ISBN-10: 1512340685

Author: Damian Hopkins
(Reproduced by David S. Larson)

For permission, please contact:
    David S. Larson
    davidslarson@yahoo.com
    www.TheJenningsPapers.com

Printed as a work of historical fiction in the U.S.A.

Cover design by Oscar D. Wright III

CONTENTS

FOREWORD

It is my wish that readers of *WEST: Journey Across the Plains*, with its found journals, will find the discovery of this manuscript about Mr. William Meeks' life as some solace in the further telling of the Jennings family and those who were so instrumental in their survival.

I will continue searching for information about Sarah Jennings, her brother Simon Jennings, and their sister Rebecca Jennings – in an effort to better learn what became of their lives.

Hopefully, I will discover enough of their continued pasts to put together their meaningful stories. I too have become taken with their lives and wish to share more with readers.

Should you discover some information concerning the Jennings, please contact me.

David S. Larson

DEDICATION

To Mr. William Meeks,
your life is an inspiration for all to follow.

To the Jennings family,
your story will live on through these pages.

To John Larson, great grandfather and
adventurer, and high bidder of the Jennings
Papers at an auction in Sacramento in 1892.

Thank you.

Take me out of this dull world,
for I would ride with you
upon the wind and dance upon the
mountains like a flame!

- Yeats -

I
AUTHOR'S NOTE

In late 2013, following the publication of *WEST: Journey Across the Plains*, readers began to inquire as to the fate of the remaining family of stalwart souls who survived in the Jennings' journals, and those who helped them find each other.

I searched archived news reports, most often in California, for any word of Sarah, Simon, or Rebecca Jennings. I found a few random articles and news reports, but nothing of sustained significance.

Then to my delight, I discovered an unpublished manuscript from 1867, written in longhand by a Mr. Damian Hopkins, a young reporter for the *Daily Examiner*, a San Francisco newspaper that went out of print in 1889. These papers, discovered in a small dusty tin box, survived a bankruptcy, fires, earthquakes, and the damages of time.

Had not some intern from a local college catalogued the papers so that I might find them, this publication would not have taken flight. That so much needed to come together to tell this story is extraordinary - not unlike the life of Mr. William Meeks.

The manuscript and notes are from interviews Damian Hopkins conducted with Mr. William Meeks during the months of June to August 1867. It appears Hopkins was readying to have them published, but some fate altered that course, and so I have taken up his cause.

In addition to the interviews, the following pages impart personal annotations from Mr. Meeks and Mr. Hopkins. Many of the documents were faded, almost to the point of being unrecognizable. Where there was not enough to make out, I improvised the meanings in a few passages. Otherwise, I reproduced the papers here, as written, with great care - with its odd phrasing, a few typos and different punctuation used at the time.

Little is known of Mr. Meeks other than his mention in Sarah Jennings' journals. He left no family to carry his name. Yet, his impact was felt by so many lives across the U.S. continent. I hope his story touches yours, as it did mine.

David S. Larson

*I hope I shall possess firmness
and virtue enough to maintain
what I consider the most enviable
of all titles - the character of an
honest man.*

- George Washington -

2

A NOTE FROM MR. MEEKS

At the insistence of Miss Sarah Jennings - I still cannot abide calling her by her wedded name - I have met with Damian Hopkins of the *San Francisco Daily Examiner*. He is a young reporter for the newspaper who has been tasked to scribe my life's story, such as it is. And a promise given to Miss Sarah Jennings is a promise I forever keep.

I do not find my life to be of significance. I believe my days to be filled only with the necessity of survival in this world and in those times. And so, with some unease, I will tell of my life and my quests. She asked also that I speak of my son, Waiting Hawk, and of his life. This I do without reserve - for he left a deep mark on me and all who knew him.

I have visited upon his last resting place twice since that dark day of July 31, 1852. I know his spirit now abides with his mother's in the great open sky.

To Waiting Hawk, my only seed, I will see you soon. We shall gather together as father and son as you have much remaining to teach me. And so, I offer these passages of my life and yours, to your memory.

William Meeks

Our first teacher is our own heart.

- Cheyenne Indian Saying -

3

DAMIAN HOPKINS' MESSAGE

San Francisco, California. June 3, 1867.

Interview with a Mr. William Meeks of unknown origin.

By Damian Hopkins, 20 years of age, a reporter for the *Daily Examiner*.

I have been engaged by a wealthy unnamed benefactor to write of Mr. Meeks' life. And should this story be published, which I find doubtful, I am to give whatever arises from its commerce to this benefactor's charity.

Of note before I begin - I already do not hold a high opinion of the nature of men of Mr. William Meeks' character. He appears to be much like many of these rugged mountain men - heavy beard, weathered skin, untamed hair, and forever a rifle or knife at the ready. Such weapons are unneeded in these times. We live in an ordered world now, the great Civil War behind us, and an assassinated president two years past. And in all regards, we are in no further need of assistance from his kind.

I am being paid handsomely for this effort, and as such, I will render my best into the telling of his story. He will no doubt recount his life using harsh language and speak of his savage acts disguised as bravery. Truth be told, I dread the encounters I am to have with him and wish to be done with this matter in haste.

Damian Hopkins

Whosoever, in writing
a modern history,
shall follow truth too near the heels,
it may happily strike out his teeth.

- Sir Walter Raleigh -

4
MEEKS' EARLY YEARS
By Damian Hopkins

FOR our first interview, we met in the Occidental Hotel lobby in San Francisco on June 1, 1867. After some forced pleasantries, Mr. Meeks began his story.

"I was born in Lake Champlain, New York on June 18, 1812. That be the day when the United States of America declared war against Great Britain and Ireland - now known as the War of 1812. I was an only child. My parents, Thomas and Dorothy Meeks, held forth a large farm with some dairy cattle and apple orchards near Lake Champlain. My father's family came from England, and my mother from Belgium. As the lake was a prominent body of water for the transport of goods, it became an important waterway for both sides of the war.

"As was my duty, I worked on the farm. And unlike many children living about the lakes, my parents saw to it that I learned my letters and numbers. My father told me how soldiers put upon our farm during the war. He would often regale me about a time, in July of 1813, when our home, orchards, and dairy cows were sacked by the British, who then took some measure of control over the lake."

Meeks reached into his boot and pulled out a large knife, using the tip to clean his fingernails. I looked about to see if other guests may be alarmed.

"At the age of eight, in 1820, I witnessed the opening of the Champlain Canal which connected the lake to the Hudson River. Large vessels steamed into the lake. My father began new commerce with many merchants and traders from the north and south coming, and our family greatly prospered. I was taken more with the wondrous tales these men brought with them. Oft times I would stay long into the night at their camps and listen to their stories of far off lands, and the many exotic beasts and people they encountered.

"The weekly Vermont Gazette began publishing ten years later in 1830 and right off I became a reader. I longed for news of the world beyond the lake - something more than apples and milk. When I read of the Indian Removal Act of May 28, 1830, I departed from my home and joined the U.S. Army two weeks prior to my 18th year.

"I was astute with animal husbandry of milk cows, and the handling of horses mostly - and determined to make the passage of southern Indians to their new lands west of the Mississippi of a peaceful accord. Reports told of the wonders of their cultures and the adventures waiting for all who aided in their move. I was unaware of what was to come, as I was young and unknowing."

He went on to tell me how we grew up with the Abenaki Indians and participated in their yearly July eel harvest on the lake. Young William became friends with many of their tribe, most notably one known as Deep Water, a tribal member of his age.

"I would often hunt and trap with him. He taught me of his language and customs, and I learned him of mine. When I was 14, Strange Buffalo, an elder of the tribe, brought me on a quest into the wilderness where I envisioned many wondrous things. Soon after, I took the Indian name Dark Path and became blood brothers with Deep Water."

Meeks continued, "It was a sorrowful day when I departed Lake Champlain for the Army. I know not why I was so restless and yearning to leave behind my family and their commerce, as it was all promised to me. They would have chosen me to stay, for my hands and strong body would be of great help. Alas, I wanted more in my life, even though I could not voice the desires of my youth more profoundly."

*   *   *

Note: Our first day ended with this task more than I supposed as Mr. Meeks speaks with an eloquence not found in men of his kind. I expect that to change as he continues his tale. Meeks does hold some measure of humble manner which belies dishonesty. I trust he will further the tale of his life without reservation.

All you need for happiness is a good gun, a good horse, and a good wife.

- Daniel Boone -

5

LOVE AND TEARS
By Damian Hopkins

Note: As we met this Tuesday, June 4, 1867 for the second time in the Occidental Hotel lobby, I looked at Mr. William Meeks somewhat anew. He is a man of common stature, gaunt, with a trimmed beard and dark eyes. Mountain men such as he do not commonly live to his 55 years. On his neck, hands and face are scars of sundry lengths and shapes. I can scarcely envisage what other carnage hides beneath his simple leather trappings.

During our discourse, I will enquire after each to further in the telling of his many encounters. I wish for his continued truthful regaling of his journeys and not the blustery banter of which I have oft come upon from men of his ilk.

* * *

MR. Meeks began our talk today with some measure of melancholy. "I received a letter yesterday from Miss Jennings," he began. "Her husband is in ill health and may pass quickly. Amidst her calamity, she urged I speak to you plainly and at length of the one woman I loved - who also bore a son to me."

Meeks took a deep breath and paused. I asked that he carry on.

"I think of her often, chiefly when the days are so long as they are now. And not long only in daylight, save for the passing of time. I met her some 37 years ago after a brief stay in the Army."

Meeks stopped again and I discerned he was at odds with continuing his tale. I altered our discussion and asked him again about his time in the Army.

"Straight off after I departed Lake Champlain and joined the Army, I was billeted out to St. Augustine, Florida. We were each given muskets and trained properly in their use, I most proficient in loading and the discharge, awarded the marksman of my unit. When it came to the handling of mounts, others did not best me, and as such, unlike the other men, I was also given a horse. I was most grateful for my years with the Abenaki and Deep Water. Our days together taught me much in the ways of beasts of burden, the hunt, how to live off the land, and the honor and respect of nature."

He paused briefly, stood and stretched, a low moan escaping him. I urged he continue.

"In St. Augustine, we spent some days in the preparation and training for the Indian Removal Act. Then we were off to transport many tens of thousands of Indians of the five civilized tribes from the south to the designated Indian Territory, west of the Arkansas Territory. My notion was to aid in this effort for some years, and in so doing, see much of this country - and then with some thought, come upon my next venture."

I asked if he then witnessed what is now called
The Trail of Tears and the mistreatment and death of
so many Indians.

He went to the window, pausing for many
moments, his head bowed, I think in shame. Finally,
he said in a whisper, "Yes. Twice."

I asked that he speak of what he could.

"My first assignment was to Jackson, Mississippi
where our brigade removed some 1,000 Choctaw from
their nearby dwellings, taking them to Fort Towson.
After my years with the Abenaki Indians in Lake
Champlain, my sergeant witnessed my attempt to
sign with some of the Choctaw and understand their
language. The commander of our brigade, a Colonel
Masterson, positioned me as interpreter where I was
instructed to learn their words and customs. I then
would go with small assemblies of armed soldiers to
Choctaw lodgings where they were forced from their
homes.

"Their possessions were loaded without regard onto wagons. Choctaw who resisted were oft times beaten, placed in custody, put in irons, and then into barred wagons for transport. Aside from their wounds, it was the look in their eyes, the look of not understanding their fate that bothered me most."

I asked if that included women and children.

Mr. Meeks returned to his chair. He nodded and gave a mournful, "Yes."

I queried him about his journey to Fort Towson.

"I will speak most to our arrival as there were many actions I cannot abide the retelling, their memory still too heavy. We came to Fort Towson in late October 1830. Of the 1,000 Choctaw who began our passage, some 150 did not survive, most succumbing to fevers and disease - others at the hands of soldiers. For my part I was nearly discharged."

I asked what happened and Meeks took pause again, moved in his chair to a better position, and drew in a deep breath.

"We halted in Camden for supplies and rest, some six days out from Fort Towson. Late that night, I heard a commotion and came upon soldiers who had surrounded a group of six young teen Choctaw, taunting them with bayonets. I stepped forth to challenge their play and was driven off as the soldiers set upon me. I suffered a wound to my head from the butt of a rifle, and my ribs from their boots.

"I was called to Colonel Masterson's tent the next morning and told my position in our brigade had been changed. He said, 'You are to interpret only. Do not attend to any other military matters. Is that understood, Private Meeks?' Those words cast a firm resolve in me. Upon completion of our journey to Fort Towson, that very night, I took my pay, my horse, and my musket, and quietly departed."

Meeks looked hard at me, knowing my next question.

He continued, "Yes, I deserted. I do not carry a shame with me for this deed. Some others in my life, yes - not this. I did serve again in the Army in many ways in my latter years."

He halted again and I pressed him for where he went after leaving the Army.

"Next, I rode north to Fort Smith and from there, far east to Guntersville, Alabama, a town with small encampments of Cherokee nearby. While foraging near the Tennessee River, I sighted Indian women tending to the washing of garments in the water. A young girl of 15 years drew my eyes. And when she looked to me, I was struck."

I asked how he came to meet her.

"As I knew some of the Choctaw ways and language, and furthermore of the Abenaki, they invited me to stay for a time. Her name was - the English words are wrong - this I can say - Fierce Moon. She smote my heart with her dark hair, deep eyes, small stature, and fierce manner, akin to her name. Her father, Red Wind, one of the elders, blessed our union.

"On what you would call our wedding day, she was clad in garments of the finest decoration." He paused and a wistful look washed over him. "She was the first woman I held close, and like her name, I loved her fiercely. We lived in a fine lodge and loved well for many months. And then in October 1831, a son was born to us."

I questioned what became of them.

He halted for a long moment. "I will come to that."

He spoke further of his life with the Cherokee and how within a few months he learned their language and customs, Fierce Moon and Red Wind teaching him. He would often interpret and speak on their behalf when dealing with the government and other white men. He had taken the name William Champlain and grew a beard to lessen possible queries into his past, most notably his desertion from the Army.

6

INDIAN LIFE
By Damian Hopkins

Note: We did not meet for two days, until June 6, 1867. Mr. Meeks explained that his health was waning. Not an excuse, only a reason. And for someone of his 55 advanced years, I understand. Much like all there is about this man - he speaks plainly yet hides some dark hurt from his past, nothing any medicine can cure.

* * *

AS we sat in a recess in the finery of the Occidental Hotel lobby, Meeks asked, "What were we last speaking of?"

I looked to my notes and reminded him we were talking of his time with the Cherokee and his wife, Fierce Moon.

"Ah, and our son." He smiled. "The name given him first was Small Dog, as he stayed to his hands and knees for many months past standing and would chase the camp dogs."

That was Meeks' first smile since we met. I asked how long he stayed with them, remarking it was a long distance between a Guntersville, Alabama encampment of Cherokee in 1831 and the Occidental Hotel lobby in San Francisco today in 1867.

Meeks answered, "For me, distance is measured longer in years than miles - and by the loss of those who are no more. Their passing lengthens each mile."

His manner became morose and as I waited for him to continue, I asked for coffee service. After it arrived, he continued.

"In early September 1832, Fierce Moon was to bring forth another child to us. She suffered mightily and could not deliver, even with much aid from midwives and the shaman. And so her life was forfeit and that also of another son."

Meeks stared long at his hands and then looked up. "Have you ever lost someone so dear, Mr. Hopkins?"

I was taken aback by his query, as I was the reporter who always asked the questions. I told him I had not.

He continued, "It leaves a mark that goes only deeper as years pass, becoming so much of you that you cannot take breath without feeling it."

I asked what happened next to him and of his son Small Dog.

"As I was ill-prepared to rear a young boy by myself, Many Flowers, a daughter of Red Wind, came forth and offered to take Small Dog into her lodge. It was best for him. I told Red Wind this was good, and that I would oft visit in the coming years until Small Dog came of age following his vision quest. There I would let him conclude his situation - whether to stay with the Cherokee or come with me. Red Wind saw the wisdom of it.

"I waited until spring before departing and then headed west where I wandered as a trapper in lands beyond what is now called Kansas, learning the ways of mountain men. I had pause to go back to Lake Champlain, yet I knew my destiny lay elsewhere. I fared well, my time with the Abenaki and Cherokee teaching me much of the ways of a good hunter and how to live upon the land. There at only 20, I was both a father and a widower. That hung on my person like wet buffalo hide and advanced my age quickly."

I asked what he did over those years and if he reclaimed his son.

Meeks grinned, "Mr. Hopkins, an improved question may be, what did I not do?" He laughed, for the first time. "It was 1833 when my wife passed and I left my son behind, that some 15 years before gold was found in California. Do you know what San Francisco was about in 1848?"

I confessed I had only heard about its early days and had come to San Francisco two years prior in 1865.

"As a young Simon Jennings once said best, 'It was a brisk place.' "

I tried to hide my embarrassment, since it was Simon Jennings who employed me to write of Mr. Meeks' life. I asked after 'this Simon Jennings.'

Meeks answered, "He and his sisters, Sarah and Rebecca, are the cause of my long life, giving me new purpose - and also my deepest of sorrows. Alas, I will also come to that another time."

He looked toward the window to the bustling street and I noticed his mind wander to another time. A constable walked past and a memory creased Meeks' brow. I waited long moments until I asked if we should continue.

He spoke slowly as if drawing the memory from a deep well, "San Francisco was arising quickly and burning down nigh as fast. In 1848 there were 2,000 folk living here - a year later, some 20,000. There was no law. The few constables were nothing more than old men with hats and sticks."

I asked what he remembered.

Meeks nodded when he recalled, "It was early 1852." He pointed down the street. "Once there stood the Bilbray Hotel with all its finery, and the Jennings Theater - long since taken by fire. Alas, I am getting ahead of my story again. May we continue tomorrow?"

I stood, we shook firm hands, and he was off to some other purpose.

All who have died are equal.

- Comanche Indian saying -

7
MOUNTAIN MAN, SOLDIER
By Damian Hopkins

Note: I presented the first three chapters of Mr. Meeks' story to my editor, Mr. Brewster at the *Daily Examiner*. He was at first taken aback that I would write such a lengthy tome about an unknown mountain man.

It took much urging on my part to persuade him to allow my continuation. For that I am grateful - and also for the moneys I now receive from Simon Jennings for this task.

*   *   *

M R. Meeks started our session today on June 7, 1867, stating humbly, "No doubt you have already discerned, I am a man of little property, however. I have prospered in many ways. I have seen much of this world, such as it is, in its finest and in its darkest. And in doing so, I have traversed many places and peoples, too countless to mention here - and had cause to throw down against other men."

I asked about the darkness of which he spoke and his taking of other men's lives.

He nodded without apology, and as always, spoke each word unhastened and thoughtful. "I have done so -never to appease my own blood lust or anger, only to avenge some wrong, or shield others from being set upon. I do not hold these acts to be of any merit or bravery. The taking of a man's life, no matter the cause, is akin to losing a part of one's self. There is less of you in advancing years and a hardness clouds your sky, making deep love not possible."

I was surprised by his profound answer. I asked after his other stays in the Army.

"I slay many for my country. As I told of before, I did attend to other matters in the defense of these United States. Some two wars and many skirmishes."

I asked which ones.

"The first was the War of Independence from
Mexico. I was 24 and working a ranch outside of
Beaumont, Texas - as what you might call a cowboy.
When I heard of the Goliad Massacre of 400 Texans
in March of 1836, as with many others from ranches
and farms nearby, I took up arms and united with
thousands of Texans a few days before April 21st.
Sam Houston then led us to defeat General Antonio
López de Santa Anna, now known widely as the
Battle of San Jacinto.

"It was my first foray and I felled many
Mexicans from afar with my Hawken rifle. The air
was thick with gun smoke and death. When we
ceased fire 20 minutes later, more than 600 Mexicans
lay dead and we surrounded some 700 more. We were
put upon hard not to kill them for their cruel acts at
Goliad. When the Mexicans threw down their swords
and rifles and stood before us in their frayed uniforms

among all their dead, Sam Houston urged us to stay
our anger.

"I still recall his words. 'Today we have taken
these lands as ours forever. There is no more need of
war. The blood of those Texicans who died before
today - at the Alamo - at Goliad - they do not despoil
the ground, they enrich it.' That day for me was filled
with much pride. Far beyond any other for these
United States."

I asked after Meeks' other times he mentioned of
stays in the Army. He said he would attend to those
at another occasion. As a means to obtain more of
Meeks' history, I asked after the scars on his person
and to which cause they belonged. He seemed to find
that amusing, and smiled when he looked at my
smooth, uncalloused hands.

"In that battle, a bullet grazed my jaw," Meeks
stated, turning his head and parting his beard to
expose a two-inch scar on the left side of his face.
"Now, let me see," he pondered as he studied old

wounds on his hands. A slight smile came upon his
face as a memory took hold. "Oh, this here," he
pointed to the back of his left hand at a deep round
scar. "I was 14 and a misstep by Deep Water, my
blood brother, caused a lance to pierce my hand. To
seal the wound, a fire knife was used - the most
troubling discomfort in my life, save these old knees."
Meeks patted his legs and shook his head, again with
a grin.

I questioned him about his life as a mountain
man.

"It is a solitary way. It was best for me at that
time as I had much to dwell upon with Fierce Moon
and my unborn son's passing. I gathered some small
wealth with the trading of pelts and skins. Aloneness
is not my way. My spirit is not that dim, and I found
the need for the company of others.

"Thus, in 1836, two years after the Battle of
Jacinto, I returned to Guntersville and the Cherokee,
Small Dog to be nearly five years, my intent to spend

some length of time together. Alas, they were gone. I asked after their station and was told they had been removed to the Indian Territory some two months prior. Having witnessed the tragic treatment of the Choctaw, I hastened to find them."

Meeks paused for long moments before he began again, his head bowed, and his voice low.

"I followed their trail and found many of their dead, cast aside without regard. My purpose then turned to give each their proper rest with pyres befitting their tribe. Their numbers, however, were too great. Then a rage set in me, and a fear that I would not find Small Dog, or worse, that he was dead. I came to Fort Wayne in earnest to seek out Red Wind, his daughter Many Flowers and my son."

Meeks scratch at his beard, pausing at length.

"I asked after them at the Army post. I was met with no concern, instead only contempt when I spoke of my son of five years. They scoffed after me about my 'half-breed' boy. I was put upon hard not to strike out. I later found a sergeant at a tavern who had been on the march with the Cherokee. I filled him with drink and he then spoke of their new encampment some miles west near the Neosho River.

"I found my way there in two days and was reunited with my son Small Dog, so big now," Meeks' voice cracked when he held his hand to the height of his boy. He gathered himself for a few moments, sat and took a drink of coffee, then continued. "I spent many days with them. Red Wind, and what remained of his council, spoke with me long into the nights. Their unrest was so great, the loss of tribe members so harsh, that our time together was spent most on what recourse they may have.

"What I feared had come to pass. Their pride still remained, yet their spirits were dimmed, their possessions scattered, and many of their people dead. I went to the commissioner in charge of their station to plead for their aid. He was not in concert with my appeal and went to dismiss me. I stood unmoved and would not allow it, the sight of the dead along the trail still so hard on my memory.

"I told him of my fight at San Jacinto against Santa Anna and my knowing of Sam Huston. That turned his thoughts and he agreed to provide some measure of assistance."

I thanked Mr. Meeks profoundly and asked that we meet on the morrow as I had other matters to attend to. He agreed.

* * *

Note: I must say, I am taken with this man's account of his life. There is nothing braggadocios about his manner and he has shown a lightheartedness oft times which I find disarming. I think I can learn much from Mr. Meeks.

Not every sweet root gives
birth to sweet grass.

- Unknown Indian saying -

8

INDIANS AND EXPLORATION
By Damian Hopkins

M R. Meeks began our next gathering on June 10, 1867, with the regaling of his time with the Cherokee.

"I lived among them in the Indian Territory for more than a year, until the fall of 1837 when Small Dog came upon his sixth year - now some 30 years past." He paused in deep reflection.

"I spent much of my time on their behalf in speaking to the Indian commission and improving their condition. They were moved to better grounds with more game, good water, and fields for planting - so much of their lives now restored to them. Yet they were restless.

"Again, Red Wind sought my council as he and other elders took notice of the uprising of the Creek, also from Alabama, a year prior. As you know, the

Creek had pled to the government for their right to
their lands and they came to an accord. Men of ill
intentions stole their properties and caused great
divides. The Creek fought back, without success, the
Army now taking up arms against them. Many were
killed, the remainder removed, like the Cherokee, to
the Indian Territory."

Meeks sat shaking his head in shame and
despair. I asked what he did next.

"I could not envisage living longer among the
Cherokee in their new encampment. If Small Dog's
mother were..." his words drifted and he sat still for
many moments.

"I was offered Small Tree, a fine young maiden,
as a new mate, alas, I did not feel the stirring I had
with Fierce Moon. Before I parted their company, Red
Wind came to me and presented me a gift." Meeks
reached beneath his shirt and withdrew a small
bundle hung around his neck and stared down upon it.
"I remember his words to me, the last I would hear

from him, as he was no longer when I next returned
to them. He used my Abenaki name when he spoke,
'Dark Path, go find your way. Our fires will always be
bright when you come again. This holds the spirits of
many who go before you - Fierce Moon among them.'

"Here I was 26 years when I wandered far to the
west, into what is now called the Rocky Mountains,
and then beyond. I sought new lands where I might
bring Small Dog, should he choose so when he came
of fourteen years. Many of these paths were of study
as I turned aside oft times into uncharted territories. I
met scores of men, many tribes of Plains Indians, and
a few settlements of these people called pioneers.
They were a hearty sort and wary of all who came
near.

"I hunted all manner of beasts and broke bread
with many, most trustworthy. Alas, some men were
of an ill nature, their greed causing them to take what
they wanted at all costs with no law about. I
dispatched three such men at one encampment and

suffered...," he pulled up his legging and showed me a deep scar on his calf. "This wound from a knife in...," he cocked his head in thought. "It was the autumn of 1838.

"I was in the plains and on my way back to stay with Small Dog and the Cherokee. I sought out aid from nearby Apache. There I lingered many months and rallied with them on their move to winter lands, and in doing so, learned much of their language and customs."

I asked if he were ever in danger, the Apache known for their war parties and savagery.

Meeks smiled broadly. "Of all the natives I have met on my travels, the Apache know best how to count coup upon their enemies - and that does suggest the taking of lives. You believe too much of what you write in your newspapers, Mr. Hopkins."

Another coughing fit set upon him harshly, this time I noticed blood on his sleeve. We parted for the afternoon, set to meet again two days hence.

* * *

Note: I met with Simon Jennings to receive payment and spent much of our discussion regarding Mr. Meeks' health. He asked that I move along with my writing in haste as he is fearful Meeks will not survive to its completion.

I have never been lost,
but I will admit to
being confused
for several weeks.

- Daniel Boone -

9

CHEROKEE AND HUNTER
By Damian Hopkins

Note: Mr. Meeks' health was woeful, peaked, and so sorely diminished, that we did not meet for five days until June 15, 1867. Then he would nip at some elixir from a small flask as we spoke. That seemed to calm his state, and his cough would ebb.

* * *

WE began our meeting today with me reminding Mr. Meeks of his last entry, about his stay with the Apache and their tending to his wounds.

"Late in the spring of 1839, I returned to the Cherokee to see my son Small Dog, near to eight years. Our meeting was good, as his memory of me had not paled. First, I attended to the declining condition of their situation with so little game and despoiled water, and spoke again on their behalf to the Indian Commission. With Red Wind departed to the great beyond, I met with another elder, Bent Tree, where we talked for long days about the changing world and their circumstance.

"I then aided in their move to new lands farther West. Those months were a joyous time for Small Dog and me, as we attended to many hunting forays together - antelope, elk, and bear. I taught him how to skin game and he took to killing well, with great respect for our fallen prey. I watched a fine young man appear before me - with much of his mother's fierce nature, yet with a calmness that goes to deep thought."

I asked Meeks when he left the Cherokee. He stood, the leather of his trappings so worn they didn't make any sound.

"I stayed a year with them. Then an unquiet mind took hold of me. So in early summer of 1840, I departed again to the West. It was sorrowful leaving Small Dog - a strong bond joined us - however life in their confinement took too much from my spirit. I promised to return when I could, and he spoke in his best English I learned him, 'You will find a man when you come next, father.' I could have no more pride for my son.

"I stopped first at Bent's Fort where I had passed four times before. There were many Cheyenne and Arapaho there to trade buffalo hide, their commerce now grown to a great size. There I also learned of new settlements and trails that had been wrought.

"Of some concern among the natives was the growing number of pioneers who had cut into the wilderness and settled on their lands. I heard the same talk when I first was with the Choctaw in 1830, some ten years before - that the natives were bothersome and worse. I feared the ways of these honorable people to be in peril in the coming years."

I asked what he did next. He sat down and
continued.

"As the fort was in need of constant supply of
meat for the men stationed there, I was tasked as a
hunter for them - the employ lasting nearly a year. I
would often travel and make camp with an Arapaho
brave known as Tall Mountain. He taught me of the
Arapaho ways and their language, and as I had done
in the past, I shared mine with him. We fared well.

"Only twice were we set upon in skirmishes by
unsavory sorts and came away unscathed, except for
this..." Meeks pulled up his sleeve to show a scar of
some eight inches on his forearm. "A knife blade cut
me deep, however I dispatched its maker quickly."

Meeks paused in a memory and smiled briefly. "I
thought I had seen all before with beasts and men, yet
I was in wonder when Tall Mountain came upon a
wolf, strode to him and they played together for a
respite. Our hunts contained game mostly of stag,
some antelope and sheep, and a few bears. As the year

waned, especially in the winter months, we traveled
farther to forage.

"Before I departed to again visit Small Dog, at
the start of the summer of 1841, I passed on to the new
hunter at the fort, Kit Carson, of my travels and
where I found the most abundant game."

I held up my hand to halt Meeks' further
speaking as I had to complete my notes. I asked if he
was truly speaking of the legend known as Kit
Carson.

Meeks grinned. "Yes, though this was many
years before his fame became known. He was a hardy
sort, short and stout - a man of considerable means.
We were at once good company. My last hunting
foray at the fort, we spent together for two weeks and
our kills were plentiful. Kit was most proficient with
his rifle, even besting me." Meeks smiled broadly.

I asked after his amusement.

"Upon every contest of skill, Kit Carson defeated
me - even in drink." Meeks laughed. "Over the years

we would travel again in many ways, much like brothers. That is to be told at another sitting."

I was anxious to learn more of Meeks' encounters with Kit Carson, however he insisted in the telling of his story in his own fashion.

"I came back to the Cherokee and Small Dog, now at nearly 10 years. He had grown so, I was hard put to be familiar with him at first. When I heard his words, 'Father, it is good to see you,' in his halted English, I saw he was coming into manhood." Meeks' smile held for many moments as he allowed these memories to drift across his mind.

"Bent Tree's concerns had lengthened, again with their game diminished and their plantings weakened with little rain. As they were not allowed to move to better grounds without permission, this became of great concern and very troubling for them. I went to the commission again and with news of my recent Bent's Fort employ, received new consideration with my plea. Then we moved farther north and west to

the edge of the Indian Territory near the Arkansas
River."

Meeks took pause and sat up as a surge of
memory took him.

"I stayed with the Cherokee for two years, my
time with Small Dog most bountiful. I watched him
become more a man before me each day - stalking
beasts on our hunts, breaking bread, and playing some
measure of games.

"In the spring of 1843, after receiving word from
Kit Carson to join him on a new venture to map out
roads to the West, I departed Small Dog and the
Cherokee with a promise to return within a few years,
not long past Small Dog's vision quest.

"Our parting was filled with much sorrow as I
had guided him in many ways and with our closeness
so strong. Also, to my grief, it came known to me that
he was held in some ways as an outcast and of low
opinion because he was not of full Cherokee blood.
He said, 'The boys call me Half Man, not Small Dog,

and worse.' I took hold of him and looked him sharp in the eyes, 'The words and actions which come from those who look down at you, they come from those of small minds and small spirits not worthy of you. Your mother, Fierce Moon, was a great spirit and you hold much of her in you.' "

At this juncture, Meeks became most quiet, stated he was weary, and asked that we continue the following day.

* * *

Note: Mr. William Meeks has again caught me unawares with his tales. That he spent time with Kit Carson will no doubt engage my editor to press more for Meeks' tale. And his time with so many Indian tribes and his views of the ways West will be of great interest to readers.

The enemy fought with savage fury,
and met death with all its horrors,
without shrinking or complaining - not
one asked to be spared, but fought as
long as they could stand or sit.

- Davy Crockett -

IO

EXPLORER WITH KIT CARSON
By Damian Hopkins

Note: As I anticipated, my editor Mr. Brewster at the
Daily Examiner is now most taken with Mr. Meeks'
tale due to his stories of Kit Carson. He insisted on
my continued endeavor.

My meeting the following day with Meeks on
June 16, 1867, was fraught with deep concern as Meeks
was put upon at the start by a most grievous coughing
fit. His troubled state was so prolonged that I thought
he might lose his breath and die before me. After
several sips of his elixir, he calmed, although his eyes
were red and wild with self-concern, and there was
blood on his lips. I must hasten with my interviews
and hope to complete his story quickly.

* * *

I looked to my notes and reminded Mr. Meeks that we ended our last meeting as he was about to go with Kit Carson on some adventure to the West.

His voice raspy and harsh, he answered, "Ah, yes. I was most pleased to accompany Kit Carson as he led Mr. John Charles Fremont and his German mapmaker Charles Preuss on their second quest in as many years. With a company of pack animals, a few Indian scouts, and others totaling 25 men, we began our passage.

"Mr. Fremont was paid handsomely and tasked by the United States government to write of his journey along what is now called the Oregon Trail, and to have such maps drawn. During our travel in the summer of 1843, I came to know that Mr. Fremont's wife Jessie was the daughter of Senator Thomas Hart Benton." Meeks smiled.

I asked after his amusement and he shook his head.

"I find some humor in the workings of government, having attested to some of its good, and too much of its bad treatments and rulings.

"We were off to map the second half of the Oregon Trail. First we went along the Platte River in what is now known as Nebraska - after receiving statehood this year. Fuel for fires was scarce as trees were found only on islands in the midst of the river. We made do with driftwood and the abundant dry buffalo dung, so sharp to the nose when it burned - it made for good fires. Settlers would come to know it as plains oak. Mr. Fremont noted that the nomads in the deserts of Arabia use camel droppings in much the same way.

"While Kit led them, I would often go forward and forage for game where I had much success. We came twice upon mighty buffalo herds that filled all that lay before us on the plains, unlike anything I had witnessed before. We took as much meat from them as we could plunder. Here is an account which surpasses any words I can state."

Meeks reached in his small leather satchel and unfolded aged papers containing several of Fremont's writings. He took many pulls on his elixir to stifle his deep cough while I read the manuscripts. I have included one such passage here.

* * *

The air was keen the next morning at sunrise, the thermometer standing at 44 degrees and sufficiently cold to make overcoats very comfortable. A few miles brought us into the midst of buffalo swarming in immense numbers over the plains where they had left scarcely a blade of grass standing. Mr. Preuss, who was sketching at a little distance in the rear, had at first noted them as large groves of timber. In the sight of such a mass of life, the traveler feels a strange emotion of grandeur.

We heard a dull and confused murmuring, and when we came in view of their dark masses, there was not one among us who did not feel his heart beat quicker. It was the early part of the day when the herds are feeding, and everywhere they were in motion. Here and there, a huge old bull rolled in the grass and clouds of dust rose in the air from various parts of the bands, each the scene of some obstinate fight. Indians and buffalo make the poetry and life of the prairie, and our camp was full of their exhilaration.

* * *

Meeks continued, "My time with the Abenaki, Choctaw, Cherokee, Arapaho, and Cheyenne now gave me the comfort to meet with many of the natives we came upon on our path and we were welcomed into their villages. The bond I had with Kit grew as we learned many things from one another - he in the

ways of Indian tribes from me, and I in the ways of
explorer and guide from him.

"Late one night after a long day on the trail, and
with some good drink, melancholy came upon us as
we sat by our fire. Kit spoke of the death of his
daughter and of his Arapaho woman, Singing Grass
in 1839. He met her in 1835 at the yearly mountain
man rendezvous, that year on the Green River in
what is now called Wyoming. As I attended that
gathering before, I pondered if our paths crossed.

"I then spoke deeply of Fierce Moon and of my
unborn son with their passing in 1832 - and of Small
Dog. We stayed long into that night. This man
shortly had become the closest of men to me, like a
brother I never had.

"Each passage and turn in our journey presented
new wonders of the land, its people, and our
friendship. I was most taken with the tribes of natives
we came upon - the Paiute, Shoshone, and Chinook
chief among them. I learned of the surveyor's tools

and Mr. Preuss' maps - as all the lands were new to him. Because our party was so put in order, occasion did not arise where we were ill prepared or put upon by unwanted intentions.

"In our wanderings, we came upon the Great Salt Lake and many other marvels. Late that summer in 1843, we reached Oregon where Preuss mapped many of the Columbia River tributaries. We viewed great mountains from afar - Rainier, St. Helens and Hood, and their awe was most appealing. Fremont insisted the party move next to Alta California, a forbidden land for Americans, as Mexico laid claim to it.

"I went to Kit and asked he reconsider what lay before him, as Fremont was most forceful, yet somewhat mad. 'I do not like the look in his eyes,' I said to Kit. 'He has mixed thoughts and is unclear in mind, thinking he is some prophet with his long black hair, his finery, and his stirring orations. I see the misery with others in the party, yet they will not challenge Fremont's plans.'

"Neither would Kit. 'This is the road I have taken and I will see it to the end. Done so. Go in peace now. I will tend to any of Fremont's questions concerning your affairs,' he told me.

"You may have read, a year later they returned to Bent's Fort, many in their party half-dead. Fremont had taken them into the Sierra Nevada's in the dead of winter. They were in such low life without food or fire, that the mules who had not been eaten by the men, they themselves would feed on each others' tails or saddles."

I asked if he had discovered a place along these travels where he might want to settle with his son Small Dog.

Meeks paused in deep thought and said, "I came upon many situations where the game was plentiful and where I could see my son and me prospering. Yet these lands were ever changing with the movement of the natives and pioneers - so many ill-prepared for the kind of life besetting them."

* * *

Note: A sudden cough caught Meeks unawares and he nearly fell from his chair. We ended our interview for the day. My concern for his health has doubled and I fear we may not reach the end of his story - as we are 31 years into his life of 55 years and there is much yet to be heard, as Simon Jennings has told me.

We passed the time gloriously, spending our money freely - never thinking that our lives were risked gaining it.

- Kit Carson -

II

RETURNING FATHER
By Damian Hopkins

Note: Meeks' paleness was most disturbing today when we met on June 18, 1867, his voice so raw in its manner, the cough so deep in him. I asked if he were able to talk.

In a whisper he nodded, "Yes."

I reminded him that we last left his tale when he departed from Kit Carson and the Fremont company in the fall of 1843.

MEEKS began to speak slowly, with caution for his voice, "I wandered for some time, making my passage back mostly on the Oregon Trail, ahead of the advancing winter. I came to Bent's Fort and again gained employ with hunting for their needs. Many asked after the Fremont party and I told them only of my time with them, not of their quest into

Alta California. That is news only to be told by the
maker.

"On July 2, 1844, their party returned to Bent's
Fort. Never in my years have I seen men so sallow
and deathly. I was most pleased to see Kit again, and
he told me of their ordeal. 'You were strong in your
thoughts, William. Fremont nearly cast us all into
doom as time and again he chose the wrong path. I
was put upon mightily to aid in the finding of new
trails and rations for the men. Your rifle was sorely
missed - and your company.'

"There was a grand celebration on July 4th, with
all manner of drink and women - and Kit and I
partook of both, as much as two men could. Fremont
could not attend to his fullest, as a dark malady
inflicted him, so gaunt in his look, that many thought
him half-dead. You may have read, Fremont went on
to much fame, traveling to Washington in August of
that same year with his reports, maps, and writings
published for all to see."

I asked what he did next in his life and what of
his son, Small Dog.

He stood, strode to the window, and looked out.
He turned back to me and smiled. "I stayed at Bent's
Fort for nigh on a year. Then in the late summer of
1845, I traveled to visit Small Dog. It had been two
years since departing the Cherokee and he was to be
14 years soon. When I came upon him, there stood the
young warrior Waiting Hawk, not the boy Small
Dog. He was past my eyes.

"We both looked upon each other as new men
and spent many days in the replanting and tending of
our seeds. He told me of his vision quest and how his
new name came to be - as his keen eyes and patient
ways brought out his spirit. This was a spirit as
boundless as any I had met - and his mother's
strength lived in him fiercely.

"Then Bent Tree spoke of their tribe and their
situation, better in most respects. The Indian
commission's veiled words hinted at moving their

people yet again, and that brought a deep concern and shifting sands beneath the Cherokee's feet.

" 'I know not what to do, Dark Path,' he said to me, using my Abenaki name. 'We have become a people who have lost their way, akin to a tree with its roots laid bare, with no leaves for which to breath, or to make noise in the wind. I am fearful we shall pass without a sound, lost to time forever, and no one to remember us.' "

Meeks sat and took a few pulls on his flask as he wrestled with a harsh memory.

"We stayed long into many nights in deep commune, sharing his pipe, and telling countless tales. I spoke of the new lands I had seen and of so many wonders, the talk of my travels now being his eyes to a world he would never see - or that of his people - unless a change were to come. Each night I became more saddened than the last.

"In the spring of 1846, after a mild winter with good fortune for food and shelter, I came to Waiting

Hawk. I asked my son of his choice - to stay with the Cherokee or come with me on whatever venture we may cross. Without delay, he spoke in his best English, 'Yes, father. I come at you now. Let us travel long together.'

"No more improved words have I heard in my life. Upon our departure a few weeks later, Many Flowers, who had attended to Small Dog's raising into the man of Waiting Hawk, presented him with the finest of garments, new breeches, vest and jacket, and leggings. He stood beside me, my son of 14 winters, tall and proud - no finer man have I ever known."

Meeks' voiced cracked and he turned to look past the window in the parlor out to the street. Horses and carriages moved by, people scurried, all in a haste his eyes no longer cared after. I could see his thoughts were possessed with his son, and of that alone. Finally, I asked where they first ventured.

"With paths already made out to the west, both in northern and southern passages, Waiting Hawk and I drifted back to Bent's Fort, a place where they knew me well and where a man and his half-breed son may live without reproach.

"Straightaway we were fixed as hunters for the men of the fort. Of late, many of the hunters had been drunkards or worse. This also gave Waiting Hawk pause to learn more of the white ways. And this was cause for much of his readiness when we came upon San Francisco some five years later - and to the meeting of Sarah Jennings and her family."

Again, a wistful look took hold of his eyes and his mind wandered until a low cough found its way past his mouth and forced us to stop for some time. It became so troubling, Meeks went outside so as to not disturb the fine patrons in the Occidental Hotel lobby. I sorted my notes and came upon new questions to pose to him.

When I looked up, I was surprised to see him with Simon Jennings. After some pleasantries, I recorded his time with me, however brief it was.

Meeks introduced Simon to me, whereupon Simon said, "I am here for a few moments. Mr. Meeks tells me you are well along in the writing of his life. Has he spoken yet of his adventures with our family?"

I answered that he mentioned a few incidents, however he decided to wait and go through his years in order. I asked Simon if he knew of Meeks' other accomplishments - the fight for Independence from Mexico with Sam Houston, his time lobbying for the Cherokee, as a hunter at Bent's Fort, and riding with Kit Carson.

Simon raised his brow and looked to Meeks, "Kit Carson?" Meeks nodded and let out a small grin. Simon concluded, "There is surprise at every corner of this man. Now, I must be off."

We exchanged farewells, Meeks watching after Simon as he walked out. He began to open his mouth to speak, then checked himself - I think a latter time to be more fitting. I picked up my notes and began

again, asking after his time at Bent's Fort hunting
with his son.

"For a tribute to his 15 winters, in October 1846, I
gave Waiting Hawk to a woman who lived near
Bent's Fort. Before he went to her shelter, I said these
words, 'For this, it is best when you are smitten with
each other as your mother and I. There is no shame in
the lust after a woman's body. Embrace it, for it is life
itself.' Waiting Hawk spent the night with her and
when he stepped forth in the morning, he was fully
grown, in spirit and in mind.

"With monies from our summer hunt, Waiting
Hawk traded for new clothes for our travels - a hat, a
deep winter coat, winter boots and gloves, and a new
pistol. He now stood with the look of a young
mountain man, much as I when I was 20.

"During our long hunts, he often queried me of
my tales of the Oregon Trail and yearned for an
adventure much the same. I told him we would go in
early 1847 when the weather would be kinder. And so

we continued to hunt for the fort until that spring when a new venture presented itself."

Meeks was wracked again by severe coughs and his elixir did little to stop its advance. He excused himself and stumbled out the door.

* * *

Note: Simon Jennings called after Meeks departed. He was most inquisitive of the depth of our interviews and how far along in Meeks' tale we had traversed. I informed him we had only 20 years remaining to bring us to our present day.

Mr. Jennings said, "We must hurry in its completion as his health is waning. Unbeknownst to her, this story of Meeks that you write is a gift for my sister Sarah. What Mr. Meeks has done to prolong the Jennings' name is remarkable unto itself. What manner of man is he, we scarcely know. Please complete your study of him as he means so much to our family."

I assured him I would. After Mr. Jennings departed, I looked again to my notes and refined their keeping. I will press forward with diligence in hopes to finish Mr. Meeks' story soon.

Seek wisdom, not knowledge.
Knowledge is of the past,
wisdom of the future.

- Lumbee Indian saying -

12

FATHER & SON
By Damian Hopkins

Note: It was not until three days later, on June 21, 1867, that we next met. Right off, I ordered repasts and assorted foods from the Occidental Hotel staff as Meeks looked as if he were perishing before me, his countenance so weakened by his cough. I asked after his health and he waved me off. In his declining voice he asked only that I remind him of where we stood within his tale.

MEEKS started, "In late March, 1847, Waiting Hawk and I departed Bent's Fort and traveled north. There we landed in Independence, Missouri where much was about, teeming with many headed West. As I had traveled the Oregon Trail with Fremont and Kit Carson and was known for it, we were sought out to aid a wagon train. A Mr. Jeremiah

Foster was the wagon master and after much confer with the 32 families of their party, we struck an accord and were brought on as guides and hunters.

"When most in their party looked at Waiting Hawk, it was of concern to me, so many had never seen a native. However, when he tended to their livestock and helped with their handling of fires and other tasks, they were most pleased - and that he was learned of English, that put them at ease.

Many of these 'pioneers' were unprepared for this rugged life, coming from refined cities in the east. Their knowledge of living off the land, and the managing of large wagons and weapons was sorely wanting and I taught many in the proper use of such."

I asked after their trip, since he was ready to move on to telling of their time after Oregon.

"It had been 4 years since I traveled that same path with Fremont and Kit Carson, and much had changed. There were now small settlements strewn along our path, by and large of families who suffered a sad fate and stayed where someone in their party had fallen. Also there was less timber for fires and less game along the trail - so we were hard pressed at times. And with so many white faces crossing their lands and taking their game, the natives were becoming more cautious. At a few chances, we might have been put upon, yet with my knowledge of their ways, and Waiting Hawk's calm company, we kept trouble at bay.

"Mr. Foster, their wagon master, was most pleased as all 32 families starting on the trail ended their journey in Oregon, coming to the Willamette Valley where they sought land for farming and ranches for their cattle and cows. At the end of our passage, Mr. Foster presented us with added monies for our labors, as the families were much pleased with our endeavors - and should we ever wish to settle there, we were most welcomed. However, farming and ranches were not our way."

Meeks stood and slowly walked to the window.

"It was November of 1847 and snow was already seen on the high mountains. I proposed a new venture. Waiting Hawk and I departed within a few days and moved south into Alta California with plans to reach San Francisco by the new year. Waiting Hawk was most pleased with our plan as he had heard much talk of San Francisco and desired to see the vast ocean before it - I did also. We traveled on mules as they were more sturdy than horses, and we took two others with us as pack animals."

Again, a fit of cough took over Meeks and we paused for long moments, him stomping his feet at times to try and shake the demon taking hold of his breath. He held up his hand to me as his wracking subsided and sat once again. His voice was now at a whisper.

"We arrived in San Francisco at end of December 1847 late in the afternoon and stood on a crest overlooking the great ocean until the sun spent its last light. I had seen many splendors in my life,

however that was most appealing - and then to share
it with my son.

"We traded many fine furs from our hunts for
goods and monies. Then we took in the new year
celebration. The city was festive with fine foods and
women abounded. Of a new culture to me were the
Mexicans and we fancied their ways most in one bar.
There must have been a thousand in the populace at
that time and scores of camps on the edges of the city.

"We heard much talk of the *Osos*, the bears, a
small group of men who had taken Sonoma, a village
not far from the city some 18 months prior with Kit
Carson joining up with them and John Fremont.
There were also rumors of Kit Carson slaying three
men without cause, and I took no heed to their words.
As the tall tales of these men grew as the night wore
on with more drink, I looked to my son and the
knowing of long stories took us so, that we laughed in
great abundance until we could laugh no more, our
faces wet with tears."

Meeks smiled deeply with this memory and then it turned to a darker tone. He asked that he take leave of me until the morrow and I consented.

*   *   *

Note: I wonder after this man and the dark past he is yet to reveal. I trust he remains forthright and does not bandy his words. Mr. Simon Jennings met with me later in the day and I received a handsome payment for my troubles. I wished to say to him, and now in knowing Meeks, I would have gladly scribed his story for nothing.

Every animal knows
more than you do.

- Nez Perce Indian saying -

13

SAN FRANCISCO
By Damian Hopkins

Note: We met the following day, on June 22, 1867, to resume my interview. Meeks' voice is in finer form and I hurried my questions to make use of our good fortune. I asked what he and Waiting Hawk did after they arrived in San Francisco.

H E looked to me with a smile. "The territory was then known as Alta California when me and Waiting Hawk settled in San Francisco in January 1848. As it was still a part of Mexico, we kept low with our affairs.

"While we readied camp late in the afternoon at Coyote Point, a promontory south of the city, not far from the trail leading in, we heard a great disorder. We crept through the brush and witnessed two scoundrels with guns drawn waylaying a man and woman riding in a wagon. I signaled for Waiting Hawk to move to the right while I moved off to the left. When he settled, I stepped forth, my rifle held low, cocked, and at the ready.

"'Good evening. What are you about this fine night?' I asked. The man in the wagon was white with fear, his wife clutching at him.

"The scoundrels turned, one saying to me, 'This be none of your affair. Get on your way.'

"I could not abide in their purpose, so I said, 'Lay down your arms and no harm will come of this.' They looked to each other, then one raised his gun and I felled him, my mark in the hub of his chest. The other followed to shoot at me as I drew my pistol. However, he too went down as Waiting Hawk was quicker.

"We came upon them hastily. The man I shot had no more life, the other with his shoulder in a sorry state, surely never to raise a weapon again.

While Waiting Hawk watched over him, I went to the man and his wife.

"He was shaking so and said, 'You have surely saved our fortune, if not our lives. We are most grateful.' He held out his hand. 'I am Mr. James Pritchard, a lawyer from Philadelphia and this is my wife Agnes and our children Mary and William.' His children looked out from the wagon cover."

I stopped Meeks in his tale because I had heard many things about a Mr. James Pritchard who stood now as an honorable judge. I considered whether this were the same man.

"Yes, it be him. I then introduced myself and Waiting Hawk to Mr. Pritchard and had his party join our camp for the night. In the morning, we guided them into town, the dead man slung over my mule and his injured comrade in tow, wailing like a small child. It took some endeavor, however we found a constable who was most displeased with the two men we brought him, his jail already filled with too many offenders, many in a drunken state. Others who had been arrested were murderers, highwaymen, or worse. Of greater concern was what to do with the dead man.

"Someone in the jail knew of the men we brought in and a tumult began, one calling out, 'That be Bob Turner and his brother Ned. His kin will avenge his killin'.'

"The constable cut him short, led us out, and went to his desk. He sorted through many papers, finally settling on one. 'Here,' he pointed. 'There's a fifty dollar reward for each of the Turners, dead or alive.' Mr. Pritchard, who was standing by, picked up the notice and said, 'I can attest that these were the two men who set upon me and my family and that Mr. Meeks interceded to save us.'

"'And who be you?' the constable asked. Mr. Pritchard let it be known he was a man of the law, and the constable was most relieved. 'We have only Mexican police and their judges here for their own kind. For the Anglos and others, we have no court and no other law save one other constable, two others run off or killed, we never knew. What are your plans, Mr. Pritchard?'

"Mr. Pritchard told the constable he wished to open a law practice here. The constable laughed and waved his arm toward the jail. 'Here? There be only drunkards and killers - all without money.'

"Mr. Pritchard then asked of a place where he and his family could stay and the constable told him of several to visit. The constable turned to me, 'Now to your affair. If you can affix your mark here, I will have $100 drawn at the bank for you.' I begged off his offer and requested the sums to be used for the man's burial and the doctor's tending to the other's wound. He was taken by surprise at my answer.

"We stopped to dine where Mr. Pritchard gladly paid for our fare of fine steak and potatoes."

Meeks stood and stretched himself many times, old pains crossing his countenance.

I looked to my notes and asked if the next month, in February 1848, was when the Guadalupe Hidalgo Treaty was signed making California a part of the United States.

"I reckon so. There was great rejoicing among the Anglos, however the Mexicans became fearful of what would become of them and their lands. Mr. Pritchard attended to many of these landowners and secured good papers for them. He engaged me, and in so doing Waiting Hawk, to aid in the protection of their properties while he aided them. We were kept hectic, so many Anglos putting upon the Mexicans. As we were known for our skirmish with the Turners, we were given a wide berth and not challenged in our tasks.

"And then, only a month later in March, all became a frenzy as Samuel Brennan ran through the streets of the city proclaiming gold had been found in the American River. That he had gathered all the shovels, picks, pans, canvas, mules, and such in one store, bore testament to his sudden wealth. And with him printing the first newspaper, the fame of this discovery spread quickly."

I remarked that those must have been heady times and asked if he and Waiting Hawk pondered prospecting for gold.

"Prospecting is a ripe word for the times, so much hope and yearning in the eyes of all we saw - empty of any thought. We spoke of it some and discerned we were the kind of men who looked up, not down. Digging in dirt for specks of gold is not our way.

"As time wore on, the clamor in the city became so great that we inclined to depart. I told Mr. Pritchard that if he wished to engage us again for another cause, we could be found in the Oregon Territory and that he may post notices for us at Fort Hall. He wished us well - sad for our going as he trusted us with much to help with his endeavors.

Before we headed out in June, I found him a good man to aid him with his increased prospects.

"As we moved out, the trails we crossed were laden with people of all ilk, eyes wide, the frenzy so great for the gold, that little caution traveled with them. Everyone we came upon asked us always the same questions, 'Have you seen the gold?' 'Where are the strikes to be found?'

"We took to staying off the trail when we sighted any of these folk. Waiting Hawk found much humor in their ways. Oft he would say to me, always in Cherokee so that others should not understand, and this be my best translation, 'They run as if a wolf hunts them, however their wolf is inside.'"

Meeks was suddenly put upon by coughs so great that the pulls on his flask could not put it to rest and he could not continue. He stumbled out of the lobby of the Occidental Hotel and into the street.

* * *

Note: That Meeks and his son were present at the start of the gold rush will be of great import to my editor. There is a character to this man, which is not taken with fortune as most of us know it. I hope we can continue soon with his tale.

*Curiosity is natural to the soul of man
and interesting objects have a
powerful influence on our affections.*

- Daniel Boone -

14

To Fort Hall
By Damian Hopkins

Note: Mr. Brewster's keen interest in Meeks'
complete story has me at odds. I did not meet with
Meeks until three days hence on Tuesday, June 25,
1867. His countenance was sorely ravaged and he
carried a cloth to his mouth for our encounter. And he
took to a spittoon nearby for his increased discharge.

I would have asked after his health, however he
is the kind of man who tells you with his eyes what
he will answer. I asked he continue with the tale of
his travels to the Oregon Territory with his son. And
I wanted to know if there were occasions where
Waiting Hawk was put upon because he was a half-
breed.

H E began, thoughtful as ever, his words taken
from his mind with great care. "At 17,

Waiting Hawk was more a man than any I had met and it shone when others would offend him for his native ways, thinking he was slow or did not understand their words. He would give them nothing to feed upon, only to observe them as if they were toothless barking dogs. This was his way, not taught by me, something he learnt for himself. Had Fierce Moon's blood run stronger in him, many men would have felt his wrath.

"By late June 1848, we were again at Fort Hall, a trading post mostly of trappers and natives, many coming from great distances. What little law for the place came from a small Army encampment. When I looked to their uniforms, I remembered my time in the Army in the moving of the Choctaw to the Indian Territory - then 18 years past - now widely known as The Trail of Tears. And then I recalled those many times I returned to visit Waiting Hawk, Small Dog his name then, well..."

Meeks stood and stretched himself as was his custom after long spells of talk, and I could see his memories taking hold as he looked past the window in the lobby to the street. He stayed there for many minutes before he began again.

"The talk then at Fort Hall was of none other than the gold in California. Again, we were approached often for we had just come from San Francisco and bore news of gold fortunes. They did not listen past our words proclaiming the truth that gold had been found. Straightaway, many headed off to California with little preparation and the place became quickly barren in its residents."

I remarked that only a year later, Fort Hall must have been bustling with travelers along the Oregon Trail.

"That it was. After a respite, Waiting Hawk and I went north beyond Cataldo Mission where we built us a small hut and wintered. The game was aplenty and we fared well. By the next spring, we headed south where new prospects came about in the late summer with us leading pioneers and their wagon masters to the Willamette Valley, much as we had done the year before. Then late in 1849, it must have been November, we came back to Fort Hall and signed on with another wagon master to go the California Trail, leading nigh on 30 families to San Francisco."

I asked how much the city had changed.

"We were hard put to be acquainted with the place when we arrived in late December. From only one or two thousand people the year before to now over twenty thousand. Prices for all manner of goods and such were beyond our reach, so we camped outside in the hills. Mr. Pritchard and his family were most welcoming and we supped many times with them.

"As gold claims of all manner were in high dispute, Mr. Prichard was kept mightily busy. Also, more Mexicans had come to seek his aid with their homes and lands being prized. And now with so many quarrels over gold claims, even though many were over a weeks' ride off, he was also hectic in his preparation of those papers. He engaged us again to deliver summons and file other such papers on his behalf for his legal work and we obliged - traveling many times to Sacramento."

I asked if he considered himself and Waiting Hawk couriers of sorts. He smiled at me and his answer had me laugh.

"If delivering papers rife with argument to those in dispute and to new government offices, then yes, we were couriers. However, many times we were put upon by unsavory sorts who did not wish the work done. Twice we were forced to fend our lives and kill our assailants. One such man was filled with a hard mistake as most of these miners were oft without learning or manners. They exceedingly believed ill of anyone who approached them. After news of those encounters spread, we were given wide berths wherever we traveled. We were known as Meeks and the half-breed."

I asked if that bothered them at all.

He smiled. "That is what we were and there be no shame in it. As Kit Carson used to say when given to answer a direct retort and upon acting out, 'Done so.' And that be our answer as well."

I asked if he chanced upon Kit Carson again.

"Some four years later, in 1853, he sent word for me while I was engaged by Wells Fargo and I joined him to bring 6,000 head of sheep from New Mexico to California. There he sold them to scores of gold mining camps. By god, sheep are the most slow-witted of all creatures, so many times unknowing of any danger about them. We happened upon many fixes with wolves and natives - however our camp was good, our men strong and honest, and we prevailed. To this day, I cannot abide the smell or taste of mutton."

I asked Meeks if Waiting Hawk joined him for the venture. A darkness settled over him and he paused for many minutes looking down to his hands.

"No, he did not," he finally said, not lifting his eyes. "May I take leave now and we can begin again on the morrow?"

I told him of course.

* * *

Note: My worry of Meeks' health was increased when we shook hands at our parting and discovered Meeks' grip has become faint. I have 18 years remaining to tell of his life and I trust his heartiness remains to complete my task.

Make my enemy brave and strong,
so that if defeated,
I will not be ashamed.

- Plains Indian saying -

15
SICKNESS
By Damian Hopkins

Note: As I had not heard from Mr. Meeks for two days, I set about to find him. It took many enquiries from unpleasant sorts and bribes to come upon his small and tidy camp. He was listless and his mind did not grasp who I was and what was about. Amid his weak protestations, I brought him to the city hospital.

It was four days before he could take visitors, Mr. Simon Jennings being the first, followed quickly by his sister Sarah, Miss Jennings, coming from Sacramento. Word was sent to their sister Rebecca in the East and they await to learn when she may be able to make the journey. They are most earnest after Meeks, as if he were a blood relation.

A doctor informed me I could speak with Meeks for only short respites. He was most stern with me in

his rebuke for not attending to Meeks' poor health
sooner.

Finally, on Tuesday, July 2, I met with Meeks
again. It was odd to see him lying in a clean hospital
bed and wearing a white gown, so accustomed to his
weathered leather trappings and hat. They had
trimmed his long beard and washed his hair to the
point where at first he was wont to recognize.

THE life had returned to Meeks' dark eyes and
he smiled at me when I walked in. He pressed
with urgency, grabbing my hand, "What of my things
and my encampment?"

I told him that they had been secured and Simon
watched over them. He sighed and asked that his
hospital bed be rolled to the window where he might
look out at the city and I obliged.

"It has been years since I have looked upon this
growing city. This is grand." He sat himself up in bed
and stretched his arms above his head. He looked

about to make certain no doctors or nurses could hear
and leaned into me with a grin, "Mr. Hopkins, could
you get me some chew? The bastards took all I had."

I told him I'd see what I could do. Then I asked
if he felt ready to continue with his story.

Meeks briefly stared into the morning sun
coming in the window and turned back to me. "I have
had many hours to reflect on 'this story' of my life
you speak of, and have come to not see the merit of it.
Yes, I have lived full years and done many things.
Alas, I have also lost too much. If this be what you
wish me to speak of, then you have not come to
understand me."

I told him that I only wanted his full account of
his life and that he could speak to any or all of his
story - at his choosing. That seemed to put him at
ease. I reminded him we had last spoke of he and
Waiting Hawk working for Mr. Pritchard as couriers
- of sorts in the late spring of 1850.

Meeks took a deep breath and a smile creased his face. "Couriers. We prospered from the constant work, Mr. Pritchard keeping us most engaged with mining claims and the land disputes the Mexicans continued to have. During our travels, we were offered many other schemes - as they were not for us, we begged off."

I asked what he was speaking of, my interest keen in regards to the early days of San Francisco and gold miner ways.

"Well ... we were asked by many to kill Sierra Wimok natives, a peaceful tribe, many miners killing them for sport, others fearful of them. That Waiting Hawk was dark and wore native cloth did not halt their requests. Many took us for mercenaries, like other men of the times, and we were tasked to kill without regard. We were invited to join claims for gold - not as prospectors, only as their protectors. When we looked longer, we found they wished us to aid them in the taking of other's claims, even to the point of bloodshed. And, much like we had done at Bent's Fort, we were asked to forage for game for the large mining camps - we refused all offers."

One of the nuns, a stout nurse, came to attend to Meeks and requested that I leave. I asked Meeks if we could continue in the afternoon and the nurse rebuffed me, stating that Mr. Meeks was done with visitors and needed to rest for the remainder of the day. Meeks shrugged his shoulders in a manner I had not seen before. I was amused that he allowed a woman to rule his life.

As she set about to place a bedpan beneath him, he motioned to me with his fingers in his mouth to remind me to get him his chew.

*   *   *

Note: I sought out Meeks' doctor as I departed and asked after his opinion. I was met with severe words that he had only a month to live at best - brought upon by cruel consumption. That be the cause for the cough, the blood, and his sorry state.

The doctor did not know how Meeks had survived to this point - and remarked at his strong will. I asked if the doctor had told Meeks of his serious condition and the doctor stated that Meeks would know this afternoon as his tests had just been confirmed.

We are all one spirit spinning
through Mother Sky.

- Shawnee Indian saying -

16

HOSPITAL
By Damian Hopkins

Note: I met with Meeks the following day in the early afternoon. I am amazed at his calm nature knowing that his life is failing before him. His eyes alit on the small bag of chew I brought with me and he set about to put a wad in his mouth straightaway.

I watched him close his eyes as the sharp tobacco settled in. He looked to me. "Time's a wasting. Let's get back to it then. And forget of my melancholy remarks of yesterday. I am released from my burden to keep close my deepest feelings. I will speak to whatever you wish as I want the memories of those I hold dearest to forever live on your pages."

I thanked him for his change of heart, then asked him how long he stayed working for Mr. Pritchard and after that, where did they go.

"There is something about the fall that stirs within me the need to move - and within my son, Waiting Hawk as well. And so, after a plentiful nine months with Mr. Pritchard, we again traveled north in late September 1850 toward Fort Hall in the far east of the Oregon Territory. We had the notion we may aid with the many wagon trains headed to Oregon or San Francisco as we had done the year before.

"We came upon even more seeking gold. These were families with small children and in wagons filled beyond reason. Here were people unprepared in so many ways - with sickness and hardship that had taken much from them already and a grim sadness in their eyes. They seemed most surprised to find men moving in a direction other than toward the gold. We supped with them often and would listen to their stories. They all spoke with an earnest that could not be reasoned with, a wildness and thirst for riches as if they were possessed of some mad spirits.

"Waiting Hawk would often sign to me or speak in his native tongue so they could not understand, his finest words as, 'They are taken with a thing that they cannot eat, or breathe, or keep them warm - a ghost they cannot grasp.'

"We had seen so much in the gold camps in our employ of Mr. Pritchard, yet we could not speak to them of the comings and goings and the dangers, surely knowing we would be mocked."

Meeks brought his legs over the edge of his bed and sat up. He took his glass and spat thick brown juice from his chew into it. He smiled at me, his teeth brown with the stains. He gave me a wink, the first of our time together. I wonder after this new playfulness of his. He swung his legs back and forth on the bed's edge as if he were a child on a swing, and continued.

"It was late October and we were well settled at Fort Hall when we joined a wagon train of some forty families to the Willamette Valley. We would have moved with more haste, however three of the families brought herds of cattle and sheep. When we arrived, we were asked to stay by several in the company, to aid them in their settlements, the building of their homes and foraging for game. We decried their offers and found our way north of Cataldo Mission where we wintered the year before.

"However, every place we ventured was filled with great numbers of new faces - tribes of natives we had not seen before, Frenchmen from Canada, hearty Europeans with their words we could not understand. Of worry to us most was the manner in which many of these pioneers would take from the land with no regard, despoiling the water and leaving their cast-offs unattended to. Game became more scarce and so wood for fires. We found the need to go deeper into forests and distant lakes for our needs.

"In late March 1851, we came back to Fort Hall. There we led a small party to complete their travels to San Francisco, eight families who could not continue to California the past winter, so many troubles befalling them. We arrived in San Francisco late in April and departed back to Fort Hall in haste, the city now so overrun with vagabonds and charlatans, preying upon every new man or woman.

"Before we left though, we saw Mr. Pritchard briefly and he spoke of his many new endeavors. I told him this would most certainly be our last trip here, the city no place for us anymore. I advised him we were off to Fort Hall and then ... well, Waiting Hawk and I would see what would be next for us.

"When we arrived at Fort Hall, a notice awaited us already from Mr. Pritchard. He asked that I find a Mr. Baxter who held some news for his client, a Miss Sarah Jennings."

I interrupted Meeks and asked if this was the same Jennings as was Simon. Meeks nodded and smiled, spit out his chew and dipped into his bag for more. He lay back on his bed and closed his eyes. I sat until his heavy breath told me he had passed into a deep slumber.

* * *

Note: I spoke to Meeks' nurse on my way out and she shared how he had softened since receiving the news of his impending fate. The grit of this man continues to astonish me.

*We are made from Mother Earth and
we go back to Mother Earth.*

- Shenandoah Indian saying -

17

BAXTER & THE JENNINGS
By Damian Hopkins

Note: I met Meeks the following morning, July 4, 1867. His manner is most improved. I wish his fate were not so bleak as I am taken with this man. I reminded him we were speaking of the notice Mr. Pritchard sent to Fort Hall asking he find Mr. Baxter.

H E eyed me close and grinned. "I attended to Mr. Pritchard's notice as Waiting Hawk was engaged in sorts with a native girl, a Shoshone called 'Wandering Cloud.' She was fourteen when their eyes fell upon each other and their spirits called."

Meeks smiled broadly with his memory. I waited as he spit out some chew.

"I found Mr. Baxter, a Quaker from Baltimore, and learned of the ill fate of he and the Jennings family. Deborah, a young twin Jennings girl died when their wagon broke free on a steep hill. They built a small camp to pass the winter. Then the Jennings father and mother were killed by what he believed were trappers, Baxter's wife as well, and two girls kidnapped - the other Jennings twin Rebecca and Baxter's daughter Ruth.

"Simon Jennings, yes, the same man you know was only 16 years at the time. He and Mr. Baxter had been away hunting and came upon the grim discovery. After tending to the dead and searching for the kidnapped girls to no good end, they went separate ways - Simon to San Francisco, Baxter to Fort Hall.

"Baxter was in a state I had not seen before in a man, destitute a word not harsh enough for his situation. I could see he had once been a man of some property. Now all was gone from him."

Meeks cast his head down for a spell then looked out the window. "I have seen too much harshness in my life - in war, the greed of men, from hatred and ill deeds, yet this fate of Baxter's was a hard drink."

Meeks looked to me direct and unflinching. "I was tasked to bring this bad news to Mr. Pritchard and Sarah Jennings in San Francisco. As Waiting Hawk's attention was elsewhere, I journeyed alone. Baxter refused to leave Fort Hall as his only hope was still to find his daughter Ruth and he could think of nothing else - almost mad in his ways."

Meeks paused again and I asked after his thoughts.

"Baxter begged me not to leave, to stay with him to aid in the search of his only daughter. I have never felt so hard pressed in my life. As I was engaged by Mr. Pritchard, my loyalty lay elsewhere."

I asked if Meeks felt uneasy leaving Waiting Hawk behind, the first time the two were separated since Meeks reclaimed him from his Cherokee village when he was fourteen.

Through his chew-stained teeth, he smiled at me.
"Waiting Hawk had passed into his twentieth year,
long beyond a Cherokee warrior's age for a bride, and
he stood more a man than most. And as we had been
at Fort Hall so many times before, he knew what was
about and could find his way. To the truth, he be
more at comfort there than me. I headed to San
Francisco straightaway with my news for Miss
Jennings and a letter from Mr. Baxter."

I asked if any danger befell him along his
journey.

He paused and thought. "Yes. Twice
highwaymen lay in wait, no doubt for a chance to take
whatever fortune a family or rider might carry - much
like what happened to Mr. Pritchard and his family
when they came to San Francisco. These rogues were
not prepared for my kind. As such, I left Fort Hall
with my mule and another in tow for supplies - yet
came to San Francisco with six mules, four rifles, and
other goods."

I asked if he killed the men.

"This I will say, I left it so they would never commit these acts again. Upon my arrival in San Francisco, I met with Mr. Pritchard and Miss Sarah Jennings on June 24 in the parlor of the Bilbray Hotel. I remember the day with vivid recollection - it was an early summer eve. I had thought Baxter was in a sorry state, however Miss Jennings was most discontented with my news and she took to long tears and could not be - there is a word I cannot grasp..."

I suggested "consoled."

"Yes, consoled. The following day when I met with her she was in an improved position knowing her brother Simon was alive, however the torment of her kidnapped sister came over her. Not knowing where she may be, that vexed her sorrowfully. Miss Jennings insisted I stay and sup with them at their Bilbray Hotel. After, they brought me to the Jennings Theater for a play and much music, as if I were some honored guest. In all truth, for this endeavor, here I was only a courier."

Meeks laughed, and that began a fit of coughs, which begat a visit from the nurse, who shooed me out. I called back to Meeks that I would return on the morrow.

* * *

Note: Now I know some of how Simon Jennings, Miss Sarah Jennings, Mr. Pritchard and the lot are entangled. This tale is taking root for me. My editor will be most pleased.

The soul would have no rainbow,
if the eye had no tears.

- Unknown -

18

SARAH JENNINGS
By Damian Hopkins

Note: I met Meeks the following afternoon and he was in good disposition. Looking at him now, it is not easy to imagine him gone in a month. I reminded him of where we last left his story, him coming to San Francisco and meeting with Sarah Jennings at her hotel. For my curiosity, I asked how she came to own a hotel.

HE looked at me and smiled broadly, changing the question. "Did you see the sky last night? The most glorious sight with fireworks of all manner of colors, and the sound of them shaking my windows so that I thought they might break."

I asked if this was the first time he had seen a fourth of July celebration of this kind.

"Yes, my god, the wonder of it all. In battle many times at night I witnessed mortars and canon fire. Also at night I saw forts and encampments ablaze, and vast fires across the plains. And then..."

Meeks faded away briefly and gazed out the window, caught in some distant memory with a slight smile.

"The northern lights. Growing up on Lake Champlain, often in late summer and early autumn, during our apple harvest, they would appear. The Abenaki natives had a name for it." He paused and closed his eyes, trying to remember. "I cannot recall their words, however the meaning was akin to 'God paints the sky.' More wonderful than any sight I have beheld, apart from the first day my eyes set upon Fierce Moon - and the quiet of it all - like a kiss in the dark, with only your breath and your heart present."

I teased him and asked if he had taken up his hand in poetry.

He laughed aloud. "Never. Yet my memory sings to me oft times, chiefly these last days, with songs so sweet I must listen."

He stood slowly from his bed and shuffled to the window, his eyes fixed on something distant, squinting to make it out. He pointed, "There. Over there past the tall spire of that church, the Bilbray Hotel stood."

He stepped back and sat in the chair by the window, picked up his spittoon and took out the chaw he had been working. He reached in his pouch, his fingers searching for tobacco shreds, and stuffed the last wad in his cheek. He looked up at me like an old friend does who asks a favor without saying a word. I nodded and said I would have more for him tomorrow. I reminded him that he was about to tell of what happened next with Sarah Jennings after he delivered the bad news of her family.

"Here she was a girl of only nineteen years, owner of a hotel, very pretty with yellow hair and bright eyes - yet with some darkness that was in her long before we met. Then, of all things, she insisted I guide her to Fort Hall - and she would pay handsomely. I looked to Mr. Pritchard, however, he could only shake his head slowly. I know the look of a man who cannot abide an argument with a woman who is set in her ways. Fierce Moon showed me hers many times."

With that, he laughed freely and his eyes moistened. He looked out the window again for many moments and I asked what he was thinking.

He turned to me, "Did I tell you how I have loved but one woman in my life?"

He had, yet I told him no, wanting to hear more.

"Fierce Moon softened my troubled heart and everything there was about me. I have never felt such joy than our two years together. It is a path I seldom cross in my memory because it holds such loss - yet since I am nearing my end, I find myself going there often. Maybe it is her spirit calling to me from beyond, knowing I will join her soon."

At this I had to turn away - knowing this man will be gone shortly, and also because I have yet to find such a life's love, and doubt I shall. I steadied myself and asked about his trip to Fort Hall with Sarah.

"Miss Jennings was a hardy traveler and good company - however she can go on about nothing, I reckon like most women. Every station we came upon, she left notice for her kin. After only a week on the trail riding mules, she took to a pillow on her saddle or walked, her discomfort so great."

Meeks stood and struggled back to his bed. I could see a deep weariness growing on him and advised we speak tomorrow, yet he asked we press on.

"Our path was well marked and we found little trouble - other than Miss Jennings not accustomed to taking my cooking." Meeks laughed. "After all the finery she received from her hotel, my simple fare was, well, simple - largely beans and salted pork and any game I could forage. We arrived at Fort Hall the third week in July and were very pleased Mr. Baxter had recovered his daughter Ruth."

I asked what happened to Rebecca.

"She was not found with Ruth, who was in such a sorry state, she could not even speak, held by three trappers for many months. These rapists and killers had been dispatched when she was rescued, so there the tale of Rebecca ended. Miss Jennings and Mr. Baxter attended to Ruth with great care.

"Then Miss Jennings asked I take up the cause to find her sister Rebecca. I departed straightaway to seek out Waiting Hawk, as Miss Jennings requested I use all means necessary to discover her fate.

"Waiting Hawk was pleased to see me. Wandering Cloud's mother and father had become like a stone in his moccasins." Meeks laughed. "He still had much to learn about women and their families, especially these Shoshone. We departed and traveled paths where we could come upon frequent news and returned to Fort Hall in early August, the midges so thick in the air we could scarcely breathe. We brought a small measure of news for Miss Jennings - rumors that a young girl had been traded to a Shoshone tribe."

Meeks spit out his last chaw and took a drink. Without his reminding, I told him I would bring him a larger bag tomorrow, and he smiled.

"To put off her concern, Waiting Hawk told Miss Jennings that the Shoshone do not wed their women until they reach twelve winters. With Rebecca at eleven years, she urged us to hurry in our quest. So we gathered for one day of rest, took fresh powder, new supplies, and were off.

"We traveled long and met with many tribes, Waiting Hawk able to sign and speak after his time with Wandering Cloud and her Shoshone tribe. Their way is not to talk of needs when first meeting. So at each encounter, we sat with them for many hours and smoked their pipes, until they asked what we sought. Our urgency was thus often delayed.

"After hearing welcomed news in early September, we returned to Fort Hall where Miss Jennings waited, some three weeks after we departed.

"I explained to her that we needed many goods to trade, horses being of most value. She was surprised we would trade for her sister and asked why we did not simply take her by force. I explained we could, yet with much peril, and they would hunt us and put Rebecca in more danger. Waiting Hawk told her that three horses and other goods the Shoshone cannot easily get should be enough.

"Miss Jennings bought us all we needed and we were off again to find her sister, now late in August 1851. As we left Fort Hall, the first wagon trains arrived from the east with so many families in sorry states. We could see the death and despair in their eyes, too many miles of hardship behind them, the light of gold lust nearly gone. Waiting Hawk and I looked to each other with a solemn knowing of their plight."

I asked Meeks of Waiting Hawk's assessment of Miss Jennings and their quest.

"He was most relieved to be away from Wandering Cloud, the bright sun that shown on them when they first met, now dimmed by her family. As for Miss Jennings, he did not speak of his intentions. He followed my lead in this matter. The next time we would be to Fort Hall would be the end of September, a month hence - and with a young girl we bargained for in tow."

Just then, the nurse came in, felt Mr. Meeks' brow, and told me I must leave. He gave me a small smile, consigned to his plight.

* * *

Note: 16 years of Meeks' life remain to be told. My sincere hope is that I may complete his tale before he passes, a sight I wish not to attend.

The frog does not drink up
the pond in which he lives.

- Sioux Indian saying -

19

TO FIND REBECCA
By Damian Hopkins

Note: I spoke with Meeks' doctor and he again confirmed that Meeks was faring better, however his health still failed and in some few weeks Meeks' life would end. I met Meeks that afternoon on July 6, 1867, and he was in a good disposition. Looking at him now in his health, it is difficult to realize he will be gone soon.

MEEKS looked at me, seeing my sorrowful expression. "You have been speaking with my doctor again, yes?" I nodded. "Pay no heed to him. I have been shot and stabbed too many times - I cannot recall them all - and I am still here. This consumption they speak of will not take me. I, and I alone, will decide upon the end of my days. Let us get back to it. Now, where were we in my tale?"

I looked to my notes and reminded him that he and Waiting Hawk had just returned to Fort Hall in late September 1851 with a young girl they traded for.

"Much was altered upon our return. First, the girl we brought with us was not the Rebecca Miss Jennings sought. The girl spoke in the Shoshone tongue with only tales of her suffering, Waiting Hawk knew the language, yet not her meanings. Some days later we discovered her name to be Isabel Farmington - a girl who disappeared nigh on 5 years prior. Miss Jennings was most distraught."

Meeks stood, went to the window and leaned on the ledge, this time to take in the city and the bright sun.

"Also, Mr. Baxter's daughter Ruth began to speak and told them what happened. It was three trappers who killed the Jennings father and mother and Baxter's wife, and took her and Rebecca. Five months thereafter, they traded Rebecca to a Shoshone tribe for a horse and some pelts.

"We kept vigilant at Fort Hall, speaking with all manner of travelers and asking for news of a young white girl with the Shoshone. Then in early October, we received word from a trapper that a young white girl had been spotted with a Shoshone band some distance east of Fort Hall and we prepared to depart in haste. Miss Jennings insisted she ride with us on this quest. Waiting Hawk looked to me, and I recalled Mr. Pritchard's fleeting look when Miss Jennings demanded she travel with me from San Francisco to Fort Hall.

"I declared certain orders to be observed should we undertake this path together, and Miss Jennings agreed."

I asked what those might be. He sat in the chair and smiled with a memory.

"First, she was not to protest my cooking, or she would undertake it herself. She would not carry a weapon, 'cause that be our duty as men. And, she would never stray from our side. She did not want to consent to my demand for no arms - however she relented. And so we departed on the 8th of October. It was to be a 7-day ride, yet Miss Jennings pressed her mount hard, and we arrived in 6 days in a hard rain. We came upon their encampment, - and they were gone.

"Miss Jennings became most distressed as their trail disappeared from sight, days of rain taking it away. Every night before sleep, and often on this venture, I would hear her speak a constant prayer, *'Dear God, guide me to Rebecca. Let me find her safe from all harm, and bring her home.'* These words were burned into my heart as was her deep longing. Waiting Hawk felt her distress and said to me, 'She has become a wind with nowhere to blow, only howling through her canyons with loneliness.'

"Upon that, I watched him tend to her needs with more care. After another week on the trail, I asked that we step aside and gather supplies.

However, Miss Jennings would hear none of it, almost becoming mad with her quest. I insisted. Our mounts needed tending and our stores were low. So, we journeyed to Cataldo Mission where Waiting Hawk and I passed many times on our way to our winter camp. We traded our mules and Miss Jennings took a horse."

I asked if robbers or thieves ever set upon them.

"There were a few passages where it could have turned sour, however, we were at the ready, and no ill befell us. Waiting Hawk spoke to natives at the mission and we received news from other travelers there. He heard of other Shoshone bands and where they make their winter camps far East of here. That is where we headed next.

"Some days later, near the first of November, we came upon a band moving to winter grounds. As is their way, the young braves rode up to us with much commotion and sorely frightened Miss Jennings, slapping her horse. Waiting Hawk placed his mount

between them and stared them down." Meeks smiled
with a memory. "I saw a look pass between Miss
Jennings and Waiting Hawk and could feel a union
begin."

I had to know if Miss Jennings and Waiting
Hawk became deep friends - or more.

"Had fate not stepped in ..." Meeks looked
outside wistfully. "The ebb of life can turn in a
moment, in a breath, in inches, often within a single
sound of a heart."

He stayed like that for many moments and
turned back to me, his eyes moist from a memory. He
wiped his nose with his hand.

"Miss Jennings waited with me while Waiting
Hawk spoke at length to tribe elders. The young
children and women came up to Miss Jennings only
to touch her golden hair and fine boots. Waiting
Hawk traded for some provisions, mostly pemmican,
and we departed. They told him of another settlement
farther East where Rebecca may be. We hastened

MR. MEEKS

quickly, our vigor diminishing with a constant cold rain."

Meeks went back to his bed and lay down, closing his eyes.

"We awoke to a light snow the day we came upon Rebecca at a Shoshone camp. Almost as it should be, the land was covered in pure white, two sisters reuniting after two years. It took some time for Rebecca to calm, thinking Miss Jennings to be a phantom because she thought her dead. Waiting Hawk traded two horses and other stores. An elder in the tribe was somewhat displeased because his son, Eight Hands Tall, was to wed Rebecca in the spring. We left in haste and camped far away.

"These sisters would not stop with their merriment. The next morning, we spoke of where we would travel next, Miss Jennings most firm that we go straightaway to San Francisco and we obliged. However, first we camped for two days to rest our stock and forage for food. I watched these two sisters

regain their bond as if they had been apart only a day.
On our travels to San Francisco, Miss Jennings
beseeched us to aid in her search for her brother
Simon when we returned."

Meeks opened his eyes briefly, let out a long
sigh, and then closed them again.

"And there you now have how I met the
Jennings."

His countenance eased and his breath became
shallow. I took it to signal our day of long talks ended.
I stood, closed my notebook, and suggested we meet
again the next day. However, he had already drifted
off to a deep slumber.

* * *

Note: In the late afternoon sun as I was to depart, a
gray pallor settled upon Meeks. His cough has waned,
as if his lungs are too weak to rid themselves of this

disease that gained hold of him. I wish him a painless
final journey. He has become a friend to me now.

One rain does not make a crop.

- Creole Indian saying -

20

TO FIND SIMON
By Damian Hopkins

Note: I met with Meeks the following afternoon, July 7, 1867. The grayness I observed yesterday is not departed, yet his grit will not allow it to dissuade our time together. He waved me in the room and smiled when I held up a bag of chew. I waited until he had worked the tobacco to its proper size and aimed his first spit into the cuspidor with great precision.

I took my usual chair by the window so he could look out when we spoke. He began, "Let me see. We last spoke of me and Waiting Hawk coming to San Francisco with Miss Jennings and her sister Rebecca, yes?"

I nodded and asked he continue.

"When we returned a week before Christmas, she awarded us with further payment for our duties. I must now speak to the clamor these women make. Mr. Baxter was now at the hotel with his daughter Ruth. And with the trials she and Rebecca endured, and with Miss Jennings in tow, me and Waiting Hawk could not abide the high squeals and such. We were glad to camp outside the city and come to town for visits. Also the fine guests at the Bilbray did not take to the look of Waiting Hawk, and me, for that matter. We said little and watched much, and that unnerved them as Miss Jennings told us.

"For Christmas, we dined with Miss Jennings and Rebecca, the Baxters and Mr. Pritchard's family with all their holiday finery. Waiting Hawk and I had never supped in such elegance before and we looked to those around us at the table for our way with forks and spoons. And the foodstuffs which they presented were of unknown origin to us, some from deep under the sea and uncooked. We were most glad to return to our camp.

"Our next task was to find Simon Jennings, Miss Jenning's brother - a tall duty with the disorder in California and the city so large. The swell of this humanity reminded us of the vast buffalo herds we had seen. They grazed upon prairie grass - and these men grazed upon the dirt in streams. Waiting Hawk and I were hard pressed to discover how we would find a boy of 17 among them, their camps scattered everywhere with no records to follow. He said to me when we were alone, using my native name oft times, 'Dark Path, she asks us to find one bird in the sky. How is this possible?' My only reply was that we must use apt bait."

Meeks paused for a while with a soft smile and let the memory come to him. He let loose with another accurate spit, the cuspidor sounding like a church bell. I asked what kind of bait they used.

"Early in the new year, Miss Jennings had notices made which we placed about and she also posted in newspapers. We were fully occupied

because of the $1,000 reward she offered, many
charlatans claiming to know of Simon's whereabouts
and holding out their knowledge until they received
just payment. It was a time wrought with increased
despair for Miss Jennings. Her hope would arise and
then be dashed when we discovered their ruses.

"A week into the new year and we had a sad
occurrence one night as Waiting Hawk departed
alone for our camp, while I stayed behind to assist
Mr. Prichard with papers. I heard a commotion
outside, two shots fired, and ran out into a fray -
finding six thieves had set upon Waiting Hawk. Two
were already slain by him and we quickly dispatched
the others. Waiting Hawk looked about and found
Miss Jennings in shock at the blood and mayhem - he
took her inside to calm her.

"A crowd gathered and a constable arrived, his
intent to arrest us both. Mr. Pritchard stepped forth
and advised otherwise. As he was a man of the law
and knew of these things, and witnesses came forth to

attest to the matter, no arrest was made. A lone survivor with a mortal wound was taken away.

"Miss Jennings saw a knowing come between Waiting Hawk and me and later asked after our relations. I told her he was my son. She pressed further and I spoke briefly of Fierce Moon and my time with the Cherokee. Aside from my days with Kit Carson, this was the first time I uttered Fierce Moon's name to anyone since her passing. It felt good - placing her name in Miss Jennings' hands.

"With no good outcome from the many coming for her reward, in late March it was decided we would go in search of Simon. Miss Jennings sent notices to forts, newspapers and settlements on the trails back to Pittsburgh from where the Jennings family came nearly 3 years before. Again, Miss Jennings was resolute that she travel with us - and so we sought advice from many prospectors and planned with maps how we should go about our travels."

I asked if they came upon trouble. Meeks gave me a knowing smile.

"Always. For many who did not have the will to struggle for gold, or who could not survive the harsh life, they took to other ways. And with a young woman in tow, that added to our danger. One such - we had been 10 days on the trail and to many mining camps when we paused at Negro Bar, east of Sacramento, to add to our supplies. Miss Jennings and Waiting Hawk remained outside whilst I entered the general store.

"After some minutes, I heard a commotion outside and came upon 4 men accosting Miss Jennings and Waiting Hawk - with bandied knives and cruel words thrown at them. Waiting Hawk stood before them at the ready. I went to them and put forth a challenge which was not met."

I asked what he said.

Meeks looked out the window and closed his eyes. "Step forth and forfeit your lives - each of you to hell where further wrath awaits you."

A broad smile showed on his chaw-stained teeth. I asked what amused him.

"After many years with men of all kinds, I know who will stand and who will flee - and whichever the way, I am in readiness. These men were longing for the sight of a chaste woman, not the unclean whores who worked the mining camps. And with Miss Jennings so pretty with her long blonde hair - well, that be all there was to it - except..."

Except what, I asked.

"They were most vexed that Miss Jennings was with Waiting Hawk. That is the way with many, thinking natives and half-breeds to be lesser men, worthy only to be slaves or worse. Those kind of men I cannot abide - and it gives me some measure of shame they are white, like me."

Meeks shook his head, took a deep breath, and hit the cuspidor again. I asked where they traveled next.

"Everywhere. Nearly 7 weeks into our journey, we came upon news of Simon at Yankee Jims, a small mining camp. As always, I asked at the assay office and there we came upon his name - and in the company of others - Phillip Tanner and Thomas Ashton. Their last assay had been 8 months before in September. I was also told of an attack on Mr. Tanner which caused great harm. And they made mention that Simon and his companions frequented a whore house named Kate's Place."

Meeks smiled broadly again with great amusement and I pressed him for the reason.

"Miss Jennings insisted she speak alone and directly to Kate who ran the enterprise. Waiting Hawk and I were alarmed as we took her to be unknowing of these things. She came out after an hour delighted beyond all measure with Abigail, a red-haired girl in tow. She told us Simon had been here and traveled with a small company to San Francisco. Then we traded for new mounts and supplies, Miss Jennings paying the remaining servitude for Abigail to release her, and she coming with us.

"It was near the end of May when we came back to San Francisco. Waiting Hawk and I were most thankful to be off the trail with these two women - as their prattle never relented, sometimes long into the night as we camped. Waiting Hawk said more than a few times, 'Their words are boundless, and they say nothing, as if the sky should heed them.' "

I laughed and asked if they found Simon straightaway. Meeks shook his head, a dark sorrow coming upon him.

"I will be put hard to speak of that. Can we adjourn for today and take up again tomorrow?"

I gathered my things, asked if he needed anything more, and he took my question for more than I meant.

He looked out the window. "I would like to visit my son's final resting one last time."

We parted at that.

* * *

Note: We have passed the point of friendship, Meeks' life now becoming a part of my own. I have a deep hope - that I may finish this piece and honor him in a fashion befitting a man of such profound character.

I am prepared to go anywhere,
provided it be forward.

- David Livingstone -

21

FINDING SIMON
By Damian Hopkins

Note: My publisher has become more fascinated by
Meeks' tale and asks that I hasten to complete its
telling. He believes it should make a good book,
something he has yet to undertake.

I met with Meeks on Monday, the 8th of July in
the afternoon, Meeks appearing in good temperament.
I reminded him of where his story last ended, coming
to San Francisco after the discovery that Simon and
his party had traveled there.

MEEKS smiled broadly. "With pay from our
journeys with Miss Jennings, and with his
full understanding, I took Waiting Hawk to a barber
and clothier. They cut his hair to respectable length,
gave him a sharp shave, and dressed him in a full suit
of clothes. When he looked in the mirror he laughed,

finding a highly-regarded gentleman staring back. He was quite troubled by the shoes, his feet accustomed to moccasins, and not being held so firm in place. Also of discomfort was the high collar and tie - even so, he was determined to persist in this endeavor.

"That night we dined at the Bilbray Hotel. When Miss Jennings and Ruth Baxter came to sup, at first they did not recognize Waiting Hawk. I could see they were smitten - and he became red in the face. I looked anew upon my son of twenty years. There he stood in the trappings of a white man - yet his eyes held the wisdom and ways of his people."

I asked what happened to Simon.

"For two days, we searched everywhere, however, with so many people in the city and no order, it became a hard task. Miss Jennings placed notices in newspapers without good fortune. At our camp that night, we stood looking over the city. Waiting Hawk waved his arm across the horizon, 'Easier to find a bird in the sky, than a fish in this sea.'

"The next day, luck appeared in a letter from Simon. He came upon one of Miss Jennings' postings at Fort Hall where he had gone in search of Rebecca. He told of how he traveled with Knute, a Swede, to aid in his endeavor. That both of Simon's sisters were alive was of great joy to him. Miss Jennings, Rebecca and Ruth hurried in their preparations for Simon's homecoming. Ruth, who had been sweet on Simon when their families came west, became mightily distraught - I'm certain due to her hard time with the trappers. Waiting Hawk and I were thus kept occupied in our task to find Phillip Tanner and Thomas Ashton with Miss Jennings placing more notices in the paper to aid our search.

"Then one night while we dined with Miss Jennings at the Bilbray..."

Meeks looked away and stopped mid sentence. I asked him to continue.

"Miss Jennings had been called on many times by Mr. Sanford, a man of great property. He came in to our dinner unannounced, with heavy drink in him, and caused a stir - yelling at her about the company she kept while he looked to Waiting Hawk. Miss Jennings asked him to depart. When he moved to put hands on her, Waiting Hawk stood in his way and said nothing - yet his eyes told him to leave. He did and that was the last Miss Jennings ever saw of Mr. Sanford."

I asked again if Miss Jennings and Waiting Hawk became acquainted in a more profound way.

Meeks' eyes were downcast. "I will speak more to that later." He stood and went to the window, looking out at the stormy sky at length.

"Miss Jennings received no more news from Simon, and it was a few weeks later in June when we found Phillip Tanner and Thomas Ashton. They were at a boarding house only a mile away and had been holding forth teachings to those wanting to learn the trade of gold mining. The excitement of Miss Jennings and Rebecca was too great for us, so me and

Waiting Hawk departed to our camp to await word of Simon's return - and to leave them to their unbridled merriment.

"It was only a week later when we were called upon by Miss Jennings. In an alarming post, she received Simon's journal and a ransom letter. I believe she kept the letter. Scoundrels near Eagle Station, in Nevada, demanded $50,000 in gold for Simon's return. They stated they had killed a large Swede, Simon's travel companion. If they did not receive a letter of agreement by the 10th of July, they would kill Simon also.

"Knowing what these men were about, I was set to leave in haste with Waiting Hawk and get Simon back at all costs. However, Miss Jennings and Mr. Pritchard were most forceful in their appeal to follow the captors' instructions. And so she wrote a letter to the kidnappers and we waited. This gave Miss Jennings pause to read the journal of her father and Simon to learn of the fate of them all. She could often be found in the parlor by the window, Rebecca in tow, reading passages, their eyes wet with the memories of their family now gone.

"For two afternoons, we met with Miss Jennings, Mr. Pritchard, Mr. Baxter, and Phillip and Thomas, to discuss a plan - only talk, no act worthy of mention. I did not let on my discomfort, however I could not abide the waiting. That night I packed and wrote a letter to Miss Jennings, Waiting Hawk delivering it to her the next day."

As he was about to go on, I asked if he could recall what he wrote.

Meeks smiled and nodded. "I remember most all that has happened in my life, and words on paper come to me most clearly."

Dear Miss Jennings,

I cannot delay. I know of these kind of men. Time is a curse for your brother, so I leave in haste. Next they will ask more from

*you for your brother's return. I will not stand
on that.*

*Waiting Hawk remains in your charge
while I am away. Trust your needs to him. I
travel to Eagle Station where I will pose as a
trapper and out these scallywags. I will send
to you any news.*

God Speed

Mr. William Meeks

At that, Meeks brooded in some deep thoughts. I
knew he wished not to be disturbed further. When I
took my leave, he barely acknowledged my going.

*   *   *

Note: I can feel this passage wearing upon Meeks, as
if some new disease has taken hold of his
countenance.

The rain falls on the just and the unjust.

- Hopi Indian saying -

22

TO RESCUE SIMON
By Damian Hopkins

Note: In the morning of Monday, July 8, 1867, I met
with my publisher. He read my latest notes and
worried after two particulars - that I remain truthful
in my reporting of Meeks' tale, noticing I have
become close to him - and that Meeks survive to the
end of it. I assured him I would hurry my efforts.
However, the telling of this man's extraordinary life
takes a toll on the teller.

MEEKS lay in bed in a restless state when I
came to him today. He began. "I reached
Eagle Station on July 4, 1852 and there was a small
commotion and celebration of the nation's birth
within the encampment. I wrote a letter to Miss
Jennings. This is what I sent."

Dear Miss Jennings,

I have arrived at Eagle Station. This place has a rugged temper. Few live here but 2 dozen families and maybe 50 men of sorts camped about. I delivered this letter to the rider away from Eagle Station. He, I am forced to trust - others, I cannot.

I will lay trap lines not far from here, then camp with others and listen for news.

I will find your brother and return him alive or not. His captors shall have no need of gold.

God Speed

Mr. William Meeks

"Unbeknownst to me, as I later discovered, Miss Jennings received a letter from Simon's captors, withdrew from the bank $50,000 in gold with a weight of some 200 pounds. She tasked Waiting Hawk to deliver it to Eagle Station to secure Simon's release.

And so, Waiting Hawk began his travels. A day later, Miss Jennings could not bear the delay of doing nothing, only to remain behind, and so she went off in haste after Waiting Hawk, coming upon him in two days."

I asked if they developed a deep friendship of sorts when they traveled alone.

Meeks knew what I proposed, and he answered otherwise. "Even though he was raised by the Cherokee for 14 years and their ways with women are different, my son is a man of honor and would not force his intentions on a woman such as Miss Jennings. However, on their travels, a deep bond grew between them. I could see it in their manner when they arrived in late July."

I asked if he sent other letters to Miss Jennings and Waiting Hawk, thinking they still remained in San Francisco.

"Yes, I did. A week before they arrived I wrote her, however she did not read of it until she returned.

Dear Miss Jennings,

I heard some men talk of a large Swede who had been killed. I am nearing the discovery of your brother and his captors.

There is a raucous band of horse traders I will seek out - and as always look for more news.

God Speed

Mr. William Meeks

"Some 2 weeks later, at the end of the month, as Waiting Hawk knows my ways well, he, with Miss Jennings in tow, found my camp. I was most pleased to have their company as I had not received any word of their plan. She spoke of the gold, only bringing $5,000 with them, burying $45,000 along the trail - to keep the kidnappers at bay should their play be to kill us and take all the gold."

I asked if they had troubles on their journey.

"Miss Jennings spoke of how they were put upon by 3 outlaws, Waiting Hawk chasing off 2 and forfeiting the life of the other with his hatchet. When Miss Jennings spoke of this tale, her eyes glistened with pride and something more..."

Meeks stood slowly and walked to the window. I asked him what he meant by "something more."

"An affection had grown between Miss Jennings and Waiting Hawk. Nothing untoward, yet I knew their spirits had become bound in more than this journey. It also be the cause of what ended my son's life."

Meeks coughed deeply, as if to rid himself of a harmful memory. When he turned to me, a deep sadness filled his wet eyes. I asked if he was done for the day, then he waved me off.

"Agreeing to their demands, Miss Jennings wrote to the kidnappers that 'Mr. Hawk' be the lone emissary to deliver the gold in exchange for Simon. This then began a most fragile planning, to protect all and recover Simon. Waiting Hawk left notice with Mr. Masterson at the general store that he had arrived and to arrange for the exchange. He was told to meet in a clearing a mile east of Eagle Station.

"Then on Sunday, August 1st, I found this place early in the morning and lay in wait long before Waiting Hawk and Miss Jennings arrived. I saw Simon, bound at the hands with a rope around his neck. They numbered 6 and all were armed, 4 hiding in the trees, I behind them. At noon, Waiting Hawk and Miss Jennings rode into the clearing with another horse."

Meeks sat to finish his tale, a great weariness coming over him.

"Mr. Gander, their leader, stepped forward with Simon in tow and asked after Miss Jennings. 'Who be you?'

"Waiting Hawk answered, 'I am Mr. Hawk and this be the sister come to claim her brother.'

"Mr. Gander asked to see the gold. Waiting Hawk dismounted and handed over 4 bags. I could see the fear in Miss Jennings' eyes when Gander looked inside, hefted the bags and smiled. He pulled on the rope around Simon's neck and brought him forward. Gander said, 'Take him.'

"Waiting Hawk cut Simon's bonds and helped him up on a horse. As they turned to depart, the 4 men in the trees came forward into the clearing and I moved through the brush to the edge, my rifle sighted on the man nearest Waiting Hawk. One of Gander's men took the bags, holding them in his hands as if they were scales. When Simon and Miss Jennings turned to be off, the man yelled after them, 'This is not all the gold!'

"Waiting Hawk slapped Miss Jennings' horse and turned to the men who all brandished their guns. I stepped forward behind them. Volleys began, Waiting Hawk felling Mr. Gander straight off. I shot one and he went down, then strayed into them, my hatchet cleaving the neck of a man close to me."

Meeks eyes tightened as he continued.

"When I looked about again, all were felled - and my son also, struck in the chest. I went to each man, two still with life - which I ended. I quickly desecrated their bodies, my blood lust so strong and wanting their spirits to end here. Then I went to my son and held him, whispering to him in his native tongue, 'Your spirit is free to leave us now.' He could not speak, so he signed to me."

Tears streamed down Meeks' face as he gazed out the window. I waited many minutes, then asked him what Waiting Hawk signed. Meeks wiped his face and turned to me.

"I have not spoken of this to any since that day." Meeks paused and bowed his head. "Waiting Hawk's right hand raised and he signed of seeing his mother, Fierce Moon. And then his spirit passed."

It was as if Meeks stopped breathing, and I waited long before I asked if he were injured.

"Yes, only a scratch." Meeks pulled down his nightshirt to show me a scar on his shoulder. "However, Miss Jennings was struck, a bullet taken on the side of her head. She went down and Simon tended to her as I was with my son."

Meeks bowed his head again, his stature appearing to diminish, as if his spirit were departing as well. His breath shallow, I called to him and he did not respond. I went after the nurse and she helped Meeks into his bed, where he curled himself into a small spot and drifted off.

* * *

Note: I have lastly come to Meeks' great sorrow, the loss of his son. Fifteen years remain in the telling of his life. His speaking of this passage may well have ended our days together.

A people without a history is like
wind over buffalo grass.

- Sioux Indian saying -

23
HEALING SARAH
By Damian Hopkins

Note: I asked after Meeks over the next four days and was rebuffed each time by his doctors. Then on Sunday, July 14 we met. I queried his doctor who told me Meeks refused to eat, a sign he had witnessed too many times when a patient had consigned themselves to death.

A heavy gray pallor is still upon him. I understand now why he did not want to speak of his son's passing. I went to Meeks and asked if he was ready to continue. He nodded and I reminded him how we last left with Sarah's wound.

MEEKS stared at me long from his bed, his eyes sunken and dull. Then a small smile tried to break through. "This morning Rebecca arrived from the East and visited. She with her husband

Robert, a fine man. And their 2 children. My, what the years have wrought."

Meeks' face calmed and he closed his eyes. When he opened them after several minutes, I held a fresh bag of chew before him. Even that did little to bring him around. He held up his hand for me to keep it. I asked that he continue his story of tending Sarah's wound.

"Yes, she was in a most grave way. I sent word to Mr. Pritchard how Miss Jennings received a bullet wound and was in a deep sleep. The bone above her ear was splintered and her bleeding would not cease. I tended to injuries such as this before, alas with little good fortune. I dressed her wound and tasked Simon to search for herbs to aid in her healing."

Meeks stood up slowly from his bed and shuffled to the window, looking out at the bright summer day. "I found a fitting resting place to build a pyre for my son, as I could not find it in me to lay him in the ground, the custom of his Cherokee people. I placed his trappings next to him and offered what prayers a broken man could do in his native tongue."

He sat, his head down for a long spell, until he looked up, "In a dream, he came to me just this last night with his mother Fierce Moon at his side. They spoke of what lay beyond and how they wait for me. I must be nearing my time."

Meeks smiled softly with the memory, then began a cough that would not subside. Two nurses came to him straightaway and put him to bed and told me I must leave. Meeks was in such a state, he did not even know of my departure.

*   *   *

Note: I cannot help wonder if this will be our final time together - my last chance to speak with my friend. This writing of Meeks' life had been so profound, all else means nothing to me now.

A good chief gives,
he does not take.

- Mohawk Indian saying -

24
RETURNING SARAH
By Damian Hopkins

Note: The following morning I received word from Simon to come in haste to see Meeks in the hospital. I came to his bed expecting to find him receiving last rites - instead, I discovered Sarah, Simon, Rebecca, and the honorable Judge Pritchard surrounding him. Meeks was taking hot soup from Sarah and sitting up, his health somewhat restored.

At first I felt as an intruder, however, he waved me forward with a smile and I joined them, now part of this Jennings family and its history, a profound moment for me. Meeks then spoke of where we last left our talk and Rebecca asked if he would tell how he healed Sarah and got Simon and her back to San Francisco. Mr. Pritchard resounded and urged him on.

MEEKS finished his last bit of soup and Sarah wiped the dribble from his beard. All took to chairs near his bed as we waited for Meeks to begin. He looked from one to another with pride and affection, almost as a father would. "You know, I have traveled many paths in your service, yet you never gave me cause to feel as your servant." He paused long while we waited. "That journey coming to San Francisco was the most unforgiving, tending to Miss Jennings in her state, and leaving Waiting Hawk behind."

Sarah reached up and took Meeks' hand and he looked to her as he spoke.

"Your spirit almost left you, Miss Jennings - with so much of your blood spilt. I wrapped your head tightly so as to keep it from falling apart. It has been fifteen years since that day - does a mark still remain?"

Sarah pushed aside her long blonde hair. A large scar, the color, size and shape of a small red apple, could still be seen. "It is nothing," Sarah answered. "I would not be here if not for you ... and Waiting Hawk." Her eyes moistened as she looked to Meeks.

They stayed in that manner for long moments until Meeks said, "You fought bravely to stay alive. It was the fire knife that sealed the wound and brought the healing."

"I almost remember the pain," Sarah said.

"I had to hold you down. And what about the herbs, Mr. Meeks?" Simon asked.

"Yes, those too. You learned well, Simon," Meeks answered.

Rebecca joined in, smiling, "Sarah wore hats and scarves for a year and everyone came to see her."

"They looked at me as an oddity, like some kind of attraction at a carnival. I would have none of it," Sarah said. She turned to Meeks, "The morning we departed Eagle Station, we first traveled to Waiting Hawk's final resting. You offered a prayer to the four corners and then to the earth and sky. What was it you said?"

"Oh, I do not recall such things," Meek replied.

"You remember everything, Mr. Meeks," Simon prodded.

"I concur with that statement," Mr. Pritchard said.

Meeks looked to each face around his bed again, then let out a sigh. "Those were Cherokee words I spoke aloud. Words I wished would guide Waiting Hawk toward the great spirit to be with his mother and those who came before her."

Changing the course of our talk, Meeks went on. "It was four days later that Miss Jennings came about, however she was very weak. What do you remember of that time, Miss Jennings?"

"My memory of those days is uncertain, alas for reclaiming my brother - and then the loss of Waiting Hawk. My mind and heart were in a state of such pain. What you did, Mr. Meeks, with your balms and

care - and with your forgiveness, you healed me."
Sarah squeezed Meeks' hand.

Meeks flushed with embarrassment, his gray
pallor momentarily gone. "There was nothing to
forgive."

"You know what I speak of all too well," Sarah
answered.

"Waiting Hawk gave his life to save me," Simon
said, now bowing his head.

The room grew silent for many moments, all
others with their heads low, me among them.

Meeks finally spoke, "There is an old native
saying I touch upon when his emptiness surrounds
me. *Remember that your children are not your own, but are
lent to you by the Creator.*"

All heads raised at that.

Sarah spoke to Meeks. "I recall a passage your
son spoke to me one night on the trail to Eagle
Station, after he dispatched a robber on the road. I

asked him if it bothered him to kill a man. He told
me, 'A man makes his own arrows.'"

Meeks nodded and smiled. "Yes, that be my
son." He paused and then looked around. "Did I tell
you his first name as a child? It was Small Dog."

Everyone laughed at the thought of Waiting
Hawk by that name. I looked to my notes and told
them that the reason for that name was because, "He
stayed to his hands and knees for many months past
standing and would chase the camp dogs."

All of us laughed again, now tears filling Meeks'
eyes. A stout nurse came in to assess what all the
clamor be about - and she was pleased to find us in
good spirits with Meeks. However, she announced
our visit with him be ended. Everyone said their
goodbyes and promised to return the following day.

On my way out the door, Meeks called me back
to his bed and whispered, "Come early tomorrow, Mr.
Hopkins. There is something I wish you to do for
me."

* * *

Note: This gathering brought about new riches in Meeks' life. I can see why the Jennings and Judge Pritchard admire him so and he is like a close relation. I trust tomorrow brings new life to Meeks and I wonder after his request.

He who would do great things,
should not attempt them all alone.

- Seneca Indian saying -

25

LAST DAYS WITH MEEKS
By Damian Hopkins

Note: I met with Meeks at 2:00 Monday afternoon,
July 15, an hour before the Jennings were to visit. I
found him standing by the window, looking far off -
so hard in his thoughts, he did not know I entered the
room. I slid my chair across the wood floor and he
looked over, a drawn yet peaceful look upon his face. I
sat and took out my notebook.

MEEKS waved his arm out across San
Francisco. "I have passed through this city so
many times. It has been akin to watching young
eaglets in a nest as a child on Lake Champlain - so
different each time I looked upon them. Yet what has
remained for me - what has been steady in my life -
are the Jennings and Mr. Pritchard. With my kin
departed, they are my family." Meeks took a long

breath and returned to his bed. "I asked you here so that you may take my last will and testament."

I told him I was not a lawyer and ill-equipped to handle such legal affairs, at only 26 years.

Meeks stated, "I speak. You write. We need no more. Do this one thing for me ... please."

This was the first time Meeks beseeched me in such a way, and I could not deny him. And so he spoke and I scribed everything as he wished, many simple requests, others of a deep and personal nature. I found myself with my head bowed to my task so he would not see my emotion. When we finished, he took pause to read the single page slowly, then asked for my pen. He signed and asked that I witness - I complied.

He requested, "Put it in safe keeping for me. When I am to pass, bring it to Mr. Pritchard. He will know what to do."

* * *

At 3:00, Simon, Sarah and Rebecca called. I watched Meeks come alive in their presence as the darkness upon his face lifted.

Rebecca started, "We were speaking of this on our way. Can you please tell us - again - of how you and Waiting Hawk came to find me? Simon has heard our accounts, yet never yours."

Meeks smiled at Rebecca. "I am certain your sister wrote everything as it happened. There are perhaps some tales she does not know." Meeks winked. "It was Waiting Hawk who found you and bargained for you, I was only our party's lowly mule skinner." Meeks laughed and everyone else followed.

"His time with the Shoshone and Wandering Cloud, a young maiden, taught him much of their ways." Meeks paused and looked at Sarah. "You did not know he had been promised to another?"

Sarah shook her head slowly and blushed. "No. Yet I always wondered, and hoped..."

Rebecca interrupted Sarah's thought, "Sarah wondered if Waiting Hawk would have been moved to seek her hand. Did he ever speak of such things?"

Meeks paused and looked to each face, settling on Sarah's. "He never spoke of such things to me - until the day you arrived with him at Eagle Station. Late our first night when you were bedded down, he came to me for my counsel, as his desire for you had taken root during your travels. He asked what he should do. I told him, 'God gives us each a song. Do you hear the music in this?'

"His answer was a simple, 'Yes.' I asked that he go to you. Did he, Sarah?"

Sarah's eyes brimmed with tears. "I never wrote of this - or spoke of this - ever." She took a long breath. "Yes, the next day."

Everyone in the room looked to Sarah, and Simon asked, "And what did you say?"

"He held me close, and for the first time, I felt like, like I was..." Sarah drifted off, not able to find the words.

"Home," Meeks said.

Sarah nodded. "Nary a day passes, when I do not recall his words to me and what it felt like to be so close. I have never been more safe or more loved than with Waiting Hawk."

Rebecca asked, "So, what did you say?"

"I told him we would be together - after we reclaimed Simon."

Sarah bent over, her face now in her hands and cried deeply. Simon and Rebecca went to her and held her close.

"I would have been proud to have you as my daughter," Meeks said, wiping his own eyes with his weathered hands. Meeks added, almost in a whisper, "When you die, Sarah, you will be spoken of as those in the sky, like the stars. That be like my son - my son Waiting Hawk."

A nurse walked in, and seeing everyone in such a state, walked out, without a word of reproach.

When I departed, Sarah came to me and handed me a bundle of papers held together by old twine. "I give these to you with a sacred trust they be returned. They hold my story and that of Simon's and his wife's father, Mr. Baxter. Yet in these pages is also my story of Mr. Meeks and his son Waiting Hawk. To fully tell the life of Mr. Meeks, these may be of some help."

I thanked her and took the papers from her trembling hands, promising to return them shortly.

* * *

Note: The hospital staff knows Meeks will be gone soon so they let us be. Of Meeks' last wishes, I will speak of one such to the Jennings later in hopes we may aid him in this way before he dies.

Beware of the man who does not talk,
or the dog that does not bark.

- Cheyenne Indian saying -

26

MEEKS' LAST RIDE
By Damian Hopkins

Note: This same night, I met with Sarah, Simon, Rebecca and Judge Pritchard. They are agreed. Tomorrow they will make their preparations and the following day they will ride with Meeks to Eagle Station - where they will lay him to rest. Everything is in haste as his health falters.

I spoke with my editor and he implored me to journey with them and take notes. I am perplexed. I was born in Philadelphia and traveled to San Francisco by boat, never making camp outdoors. My editor would have none of my reasons and insisted. So, I too packed for the journey.

When I met with Meeks today and spoke of this news, he was most grateful, his countenance improving straightaway.

HE asked me, "Now, where be my chew?" I reached in my valise and handed the bag to him. He took a large wad and put it in his mouth, a deep smile coming over him. "Ah, I so missed that. Now, when do we leave tomorrow?"

I told him straightaway.

"Before the sun," he stated like he was already giving orders.

With that, he regaled me with stories of his adventures, each of them already written down. The hope in Meeks' eyes has been rekindled. I trust we can make it to Eagle Station before he passes.

* * *

At daybreak, we assembled in front of the Occidental Hotel. We are a party of eight, Simon's friend Phillip Tanner joining us and a rugged guide by the name of Clint Hooper. The trail to Eagle Station is well marked and few dangers should confront us.

Phillip's wife Martha and their two children were there to see us off, as was Ruth, Simon's wife. Rebecca's husband and children were present as well.

The party gathered sixteen mules, a buckboard drawn by four others, and supplies for six weeks. I did not realize the care and planning needed for such an enterprise. I will sit on the buckboard on its padded seat. Meeks was to ride with me in the back - yet he refused and took to one of the more spirited mules.

And thus we began our journey to Eagle Station, to the final resting place of Waiting Hawk, and soon to be that of Mr. William Meeks. I will now note the daily occurrences of our travels.

* * *

Wednesday, July 17: We made camp some 30 miles from the city on our way to Stockton. Even with the padding and a blanket, the discomfort of the ride has become most difficult for me. We are all weary, most from not having been on the trail for years - yet all are in good spirits. Meeks has found some new life. Maybe riding on a road with a destination ahead gives him cause to be hopeful - and to visit his son again. Only once was he set upon by a fit of coughs.

Thursday, July 18: Off again at daybreak and another 30 miles crossed. We supped on grilled cornbread and rabbit - delicious - Simon, Phillip, and Clint trapping the hares, Meeks instructing on the proper way of everything. There is much laughter and merriment in our camp, even knowing this is Meeks' last ride.

Friday, July 19: Another 30 miles and we are becoming familiar with the tasks at hand. This night Meeks spoke at length about his days after rescuing Simon in August of 1852. He told us of his times with Wells Fargo for the first year, as a guard for the transfer of gold and money - and the occasions where he was forced to dispatch highwaymen. He went on to tell of

helping Kit Carson drive 6,000-head of sheep to
mining camps. We sat by the fire long into the night,
taking in an air filled with high adventure.

As a man of his humble stature, to him it was
merely the tale of his life - a life made more stark
these last 15 years without his son. When Meeks
spoke of his dislike for the look, the smell, and the
taste of mutton, much mirth fell upon us. I will miss
this man.

Saturday, July 20: Not as far in our travels today as
we make our way through hills - maybe 25 miles - and
in the heat of a searing day. Meeks seems to be fairing
well and the others are in good spirits also. At our
camp tonight, Meeks further regaled us of his life,
passing often between the distant past and those years
we did not speak of before. Of surprise to me was his
time in the workings of the Great Civil War here in
California. He spoke of history new to me and all
those about our fire.

"I was in the employ of Wells Fargo, when
Captain Ingram's Partisan Rangers began to rob
shipments of gold in 1864 to fund the Confederate
cause. I was not on the task, however they took a
coach in Placerville with $40,000 in gold - later called
the Bullion Bend robbery. I was summoned to the
office and asked to join John Hicks Adams, the Santa
Clara County Sheriff, to go after and apprehend these
men.

"I was deputized and joined his party of 10 men.
Two days later, we came upon a small dwelling in
Almaden where Ingram's men were holed up. Adams
called out for their surrender, that they were
surrounded. That was not to be. Ingram's 16 men tried
to escape and a great volley of shots rang out from
both sides. I fell three myself with my Henry rifle.
Only six lived, taken as prisoners. Adams himself was
shot, alas not mortally - the bullet striking his pocket
watch and glancing off his ribs."

So ended our fourth day on the trail with all present in awe of Meeks' life.

Sunday, July 21: We fared well in our travels today. Rebecca and Sarah ride side by side and talk of what sisters do. Simon rides near Meeks, and Mr. Pritchard rides with me, handling the reins of the buckboard. Clint Hooper goes ahead to scout the trail for any harm, for good water, and game. Meeks continues to show his mettle, at times like the young mountain man I'm certain he was when he first crossed these trails over 30 years past.

Tuesday, July 23: Nothing to report of note. We travel well and all in a good way. Today one of the mules took a misstep and went lame. This night we supped on roasted mule and beans. At first I considered it to be too harsh for my palate - yet I found myself asking for more, as did others. This camping on the trail is more pleasant than I foresaw,

although I long for the comforts of a soft bed and a
cold beer.

Saturday, July 27: Our journey continues well, Mr.
Hooper content we are on schedule to arrive at Eagle
Station within 10 days, maybe sooner. I watch Meeks
steady himself in the saddle at times. By God, there is
deep spirit in him that will not let go until he is ready.

Wednesday, July 31: I have come to know more of the
party I keep, taking separate notes of their lives as
they each have traveled far to this place. Judge
Pritchard is a most amazing man. He told me of his
first coming to San Francisco with his family, of the
city which has become such a place of commerce, and
its start as a quiet Mexican town. Pritchard's hand can
be seen in much of what California has become, some
of his rulings having lasting effects on the populace. I
will speak with my editor upon my return as Judge

Pritchard has consented to an interview for the paper, his first ever.

Thursday, August 1: At noon today we stopped as Meeks turned aside and asked Simon and Sarah to join him. They returned a half-hour later, a sadness upon them all. Nothing was said until tonight after we supped. Meeks spoke, "It was Sunday, fifteen years ago today, at noon, when we rescued Simon from his captors. That is why we paused in our travels."

Simon said, "There hasn't been a time when thoughts of that day have not come back to me - a smell in the air, the look of Waiting Hawk riding into the clearing, his first words whispered to me when he cut my bonds. 'To your horse with Sarah now. Be quick.' Of what followed, only Mr. Meeks knows its truth as I tended to Sarah, who was shot."

All eyes turned to Meeks. "I have spoken of this to you, Mr. Hopkins. You have written of this before.

It is for you to share with those assembled here -
perhaps on your journey back, after I am with my
son."

Those words reminded us all of the grim reason
we were here. Silence fell as everyone took to cleaning
the camp and heading to bed.

Life is not separate from death.
It only looks that way.

- Blackfoot Indian saying -

27

MEEKS TO REST
By Damian Hopkins

Note: The following are the last notes of my time with Mr. William Meeks. The past two months have been of great import to me. Whether these words find their way to print or just live in the hearts of those who know of the extraordinary life of Mr. Meeks, it matters not. My life has been altered forever.

I continued these last passages as a journal, each day bringing about new learnings of this man and his "family" as we neared his end.

Saturday, August 3: A cool summer rain kept at us all day, yet it did not dampen our spirits as it was much needed. By Mr. Hooper's reckoning, we be within 3 days of Eagle Station and Meeks agreed. Midway through this day, Meeks joined me, Mr. Pritchard taking to his mule, Meeks now guiding the buckboard.

He reasoned he wanted to spend more time with me, yet a deep weariness has descended upon him. Mixed with the chew he spits out onto the trail is dark blood, I am certain the consumption now squeezing the last life from him.

Meeks knows this trail well, pointing out sights before we come upon them. I marvel how he can have such recall having traveled so many thousands of miles. His answer was as always profound and simple. "A native saying tells it best," he said. "'Tell me and I will forget. Show me and I might remember. Involve me and I will understand.' I have walked this trail twice. The first by myself where I waited for Waiting Hawk to take back Simon. The second with Miss Rebecca years later to claim her dowry, the gold Miss Jennings buried here with Waiting Hawk."

As always a surprise to me is Meeks' accounts of his brave life as if he spoke of going to the general store for supplies.

Monday, August 5: Today be the harshest for Meeks. Riding next to him in the buckboard, more than once I had to take the reins as his deep cough would not leave him. Others came to his aid, alas, he waved them off. His pallor has turned gray and the quiet in our camp this night was profound.

I sat next to Meeks on one side, Sarah on the other by the fire. She placed a blanket over him, yet his shakes would not stop. I heard Sarah whisper to him, "You'll be home soon, Mr. Meeks. Do you know what Waiting Hawk told me on our travel here 15 years ago, to allay my deep concerns and fears, should we die?" Meeks turned to her and she continued. "'They are not dead who live in the hearts they leave behind.' Mr. Meeks, if that be true, you will live forever, for I will never let your life leave my heart - nor that of my children, nor of Simon's and Rebecca's. Know that." She leaned against him.

I stole away to my blankets, afraid to feel more of their deep emotion - and mine.

Tuesday, August 6: We came into Eagle Station midday and went straightaway to Waiting Hawk's resting place. Meeks' voice was spent, his weakness so great, he could barely breathe. He spoke little during this last day. However, what he said, I have written here.

"The one who tells the stories rules the world. This a wise native spoke. Do not forget, young Damian, you can do much more with your pen than ever I did with my rifle.

"'It takes a thousand voices to tell a single story' - this, saying I heard in the lodge of Red Wind, the father of my wife Fierce Moon. My life is not my own, Damian. It is a part of all who came before me and who go ahead of me now. Do not think otherwise."

I shared a few words of my meager wisdom with Meeks, as a means of comfort. "A brave man dies only once, a coward many times."

He returned a weak smile. When we came upon Waiting Hawk's pyre, it took great effort for Simon, Phillip and Mr. Hooper to help him. Standing aside in reverence were Sarah, Rebecca, and Mr. Pritchard.

A few remnants of leather and broken bones were all that remained of Waiting Hawk's resting place. All else lay undisturbed, the heavy wood poles firm. Meeks' hands waved over the remains and he chanted low in what I speculated to be Waiting Hawk's native tongue, Cherokee. When he finished, he turned to me and nodded. I handed his last will and testament to Mr. Pritchard.

Next, with the aid of Simon and Phillip, they helped Meeks up onto the platform where he lay down among the bleached bones and tattered leather trappings of Waiting Hawk. Sarah and Rebecca went to Meeks and clutched his hands.

Mr. Pritchard stepped forth and read what Meeks dictated to me nearly a month ago, his voice cracking with deep sentiment.

"To my family and friends, this be my last will and testament. Today, I pass to the other side and begin a new path. No river can return to its source, yet all have a beginning. My river of life in many ways began with my wife Fierce Moon and the birth of my son - first known as Small Dog - yet you know him as Waiting Hawk.

"I have only my meager trappings to bequeath as instructed below. What I wish to leave in my testament are the thoughts of a dying man who has seen much of the world and lived long past his days.

"What is life? It is found in the breath of the buffalo on a winter morning. It is in the first touch from the woman you will love forever. It is found in the laughter of your son. And it is in the little shadow that runs across the prairie grass and loses itself in the sunset."

A great swirl of wind gusted and danced, rushing past all those in attendance.

Mr. Pritchard ended, "Goodbye my friends, my family."

Unannounced, Meeks slipped away - quiet and humble, as was his manner when he moved through life.

His spirit passed through us all on its way to abide with Fierce Moon and Waiting Hawk in the great open sky.

END

*We shall be forever known
by the tracks we leave.*

- Dakota Indian saying -

M R . M E E K S

Made in the USA
Middletown, DE
06 November 2020

23330045R00130